About the Author

Dr Ian Marsh has been a university lecturer for many years and has taught, researched and written widely on crime and criminal justice. He is the author of numerous academic books on crime and justice and this is his first published work of fiction.

For Gaynor

Ian Marsh

MURDERER: ON YOUR MARK

A CIP catalogue record for this title is available from the British Library.

This is a fictional story, albeit loosely based on a crime committed over a hundred years ago in the US, and therefore any resemblance to actual persons, living or dead, or particular institutions or actual events is purely coincidental.

ISBN 978 1 78554 081 3 (Paperback)
ISBN 978 1 78554 082 0 (Hardback)
ISBN 978 1 78554 083 7 (E-Book)

www.austinmacauley.com

First Published (2015)
Austin Macauley Publishers Ltd.
25 Canada Square
Canary Wharf
London
E14 5LQ

Acknowledgments

It is conventional to list an array of people who have helped, finishing with one's family, past and present, and it goes without saying that this is also the case here. Of course without them my life and this book would no doubt have been quite different.

Having said that, I would like to thank the editors and production team at Austin Macauley and particularly Vinh Tran and Walter Stephenson. Also, thanks to Laurence Hopkins for comments on an early draft and, especially, Gaynor for her support and ideas.

In merging fact with fiction I have had to contact numerous people with queries about historical detail and accuracy and have invariably been met with courtesy and a willingness to help, often going beyond what I've been asking about.

PART ONE

Friday August 16 1974

'You're sure you want to pay that much for a bottle of wine?' The bespectacled, slightly hunched figure behind the counter was clearly not a wine aficionado.

It was the same shop, snuggled away just off Pentonville Road, that Mark had walked past most days on his way to and from Stanford Primary School, when he was between the ages of five and eleven. Just after the Seven Dials on his way there and just before on his return; as it had been from the mid-1950s. This part of town was near to the house Mark had grown up in and the Seven Dials had always intrigued him: seven different sizes and styles of road merging into this small space, hardly a roundabout and hardly big enough to accommodate them all – the two sides of Dyke Road one to the shops and seafront, the other to Hove and the countryside, the grand drive to the county cricket ground, another road to the station, the cramped, narrow passage of Pentonville Road itself, and so on. The Seven Dials off-licence was just as Mark had remembered it from over a decade ago. It hadn't surprised Mark to find out that the current owner and shopkeeper, Mr Timpkins, was the son of the man he'd seen pottering about there on his daily journeys when at junior school, even though he had only ever caught glimpses of the previous Mr Timpkins through the posters and cards jostling for space on the window on his journeys to and from school – except, that is, on the odd occasions he was allowed to bring home a lemonade or cream soda. Until he'd spoken to the current Mr Timpkins on perhaps his second or third visit, he had liked to imagine that whoever worked there just merged into and became the same shopkeeper; the brown overalls with biros and glasses popping out of the pockets looked pretty much as they had 15-plus years ago.

A new Tesco had opened on the corner of the Dials and Dyke Road since then, and after the initial shock of the appearance of this brash and bright supermarket, the size of three or four corner shops, had waned, the locals, including his mum, had succumbed to the convenience and cheapness pretty quickly. Since his return to work at the university, and even though they lived on the outskirts of town now, Mark had formed an attachment to this little off-licence. He'd found out that this Mr Timpkins had taken over the family business from his father about ten years ago, which had explained his initial feelings of déjà vu of course. There wasn't much choice of wine and Mr Timpkins could not really understand why anyone would want to spend more than a pound on a bottle of the stuff, or indeed why anyone drank wine at all. However, he was always obliging and had ordered in the bottles Mark had asked for.

'You're not the only person who likes their wine you know,' Mr Timpkins announced, as if heralding the emergence of a new class of drinkers. 'I've even had a couple of young ladies asking if I stocked German wine. We never had any call for it when my father was alive, a drink for the upper classes he called it.'

'It's definitely on the up, and you're right, it's a drink for men and women.' Mark felt obliged to contribute. 'Anyway thanks for that and keep a few in stock if you can.'

He bought a packet of Benson and Hedges, even though he only had an occasional cigarette; he assumed Justine would probably fancy a joint later.

Mark's parents had moved away a couple of years after he'd passed the 11 plus, and even though there was over a decade between then and his return, he'd always felt Brighton, and this part of it, was his place. The job at the university had come out of the blue four years ago, and at 27, with his status as a university lecturer and an advance on his first academic text, a pretty dull comparative analysis of classic social theorists, securing enough for his Morgan parked further up Dyke Road, plus a decent salary, he decided he felt OK. However perhaps still not as OK as he felt he should feel. As he headed up from the Dials, to the station and then onto Queens Road and before reaching the Clock Tower – yet another construction to celebrate Queen Victoria's jubilee – he could just about see the waves breaking up the deep late summer blue of the Channel. Even the Top Rank Suite at the bottom of West Street, built soon after his family had left Brighton, couldn't spoil the view. One of the many things he loved about Brighton was the way its main roads went up and down – dipping to the sea front one way and, as he turned down Church Street, almost at right angles to that, to the parish church, Pavilion Parade and Old Steine fountain. It always took him back to his childhood: he remembered sitting in his father's Morris Oxford, in classic racing green and his pride and joy, as they drove down to the beach for a quick swim before tea or at weekends. There were relatively few cars around in the 1950s; they'd always manage to get a parking spot on the prom itself, just along from the West Pier and by Hove Lawns, then a quick dash across the grass and promenade walkway and down to the pebbles. Since then it seemed that the traffic had grown almost exponentially. The familiar green and cream Southdown double-decker buses were practically nose to tail now; a contrast with their somewhat unpredictable appearances in his school days.

Church Street and North Road ran parallel to one another and to the seafront; even though he'd not been around at the key times, they had always epitomised and signalled the town's role in the sixties youth culture, or counterculture as he was continually trying to explain to and theorize about with his Year 3 students. It was early evening and although it was still open he wouldn't bother today to stop at the only hip newsagent in town. In fact he'd got a little bored with *The International Times* and *Oz*; he'd prefer to think he'd moved on even though he still liked to see the iconic IT girl logo displayed across the shop door. Further down was the trendy record store that his old university friend Martin had set up as an offshoot of his impressive import/export business. He'd lost touch with Martin and a few other of his university mates when he'd stayed on at Kent for an extra year to do the Master's, but they'd met up after Mark got his lecturing job and since then had spent a few evenings getting stoned and reminiscing. Such occasions had occurred rather less frequently over the last couple of years as Martin's business took off at quite an alarming rate. Last time they'd met Martin had been on his way to open a new branch in London, just off Tottenham Court Road, and was talking of setting up his own record label. Although he was not sure quite why, Mark was pleased there were still a few second-hand record shops that had been hippy hangouts in the sixties and still remained the best places to browse. Come to think of it, he preferred the Record Album and the Cottage to Martin's place anyway; they were less obviously successful – and less obviously bothered about it as well. He liked the way they still kept stacks of albums in boxes outside and the ramshackle listening booths, reeking of stale fags and sweat.

At the bottom of Church Street he passed by the library and fountain and the favourite student and hippy hang-out, the King and Queens. They'd probably end up there later and at least, being August, most of his students wouldn't be around. They had used to meet at cafés and bars in the Lanes, but that was becoming a little passé now. In the last year or so he'd got to know Brighton again properly with Justine. The Lanes had changed since his primary school days, when he and his friends would take a short cut through them to get to the pier and amusements at weekends; or less often after school if his dad had been free for a late afternoon swim and had arranged to meet him. Mark recalled with some nostalgia how they had always met up at the same place and how he'd felt it was their special place, even though it was only a deckchair stand between the piers. Although they retained a little of the mystique he'd felt when he was younger, the Lanes had changed, they seemed just for the visitors and well-off now. Alongside the antique and jewellery shops, it was amazing really how so many business could survive selling posters of classic surrealist artwork and tie-dyed T-shirts, large rolling machines and joss sticks. Mind you it was hardly likely Magritte or Dali would have been too bothered about their recent surge in popularity. Mark preferred the Kemp Town area, with its mix of locals, students, current and ex-hippies and which exuded a more genuine feel than the now tourist-dominated Lanes.

As he navigated around Victoria Gardens, he noticed a few tourists-cum-students nicely underdressed in the summer evening and wished he'd put the Morgan's roof down; he was sure it was just vanity nowadays but he liked the attention it got anyhow. Justine was only a few minutes up the road. Left and up into Edward Street and onto Kemp Town, catching glimpses of the promenade and sea to his right, between the mix of shops and cafés reflecting the burgeoning mix of hippy and gay scenes characterising this side of town; and then to their apartment. He'd never found the right label or category for Justine – and in spite of trying to be a free spirit and not tied to conventionality, Mark had a love of structure and typologies and just lists really; it made his job easier, and also his life. A muse, or lover, or mistress maybe, but really now she was just his future – maybe a paramour. Even at this stage he had the feeling she'd be a challenge though. In fact he was quite sure of it.

It had been a year almost to the day, at the regular end of year departmental get together, that he'd manoeuvred Justine away from the motley group of would-be anarchists who no doubt would end up becoming teachers and social workers and sold her some sort of dream that he'd never even really worked out for himself. As he drove through the increasingly trendy streets of Kemp Town and turned into Devonshire Place and the apartment Justine had taken ever since he had persuaded her to give him a chance and some time, he felt pretty good about life and the evening ahead. He knew, though, that he was putting off thinking about the changes that had to come; and going to Tom's house-warming last weekend had merely highlighted the doubts. He couldn't seem to get that night out of his mind, the snatches of conversation he'd heard were preying on his mind, probably something and nothing but he couldn't be sure. It was meant to be a get-together and reunion with his old university mates but Mark had left with a sense of ending, and a feeling that things between him, Tom and the others would never be quite the same again.

***

Justine had lived at number 32, flat D, since finishing her BA degree last summer and starting the MA course that was eventually due to develop into a PhD. She'd never wanted to go back to Carlisle and hadn't really kept in touch with her school friends after arriving in Brighton four years ago; she made the regular family visits and they were happy their daughter had letters after her name and, even better, was going to be a doctor, even if it was of philosophy. As she looked for the petunia oil and lit a couple of joss sticks to create the mood she wanted, she felt happy enough she guessed, but a whole year had gone and maybe applying the anthropological musings of Levi Strauss to counter cultural neo-religious groups was never going to provide her with all she wanted. Sure, Mark had been really good to her, he might have a whinge about her getting stoned before they went out but she really did like him. After all he was pretty decent looking, tallish and slim and with light brown, almost blond hair, and cut quite short which was a change from the straggly offerings of most of her own age group. He dressed smartly too, usually a brown leather jacket and Levi's, and he was less than five years older than Justine. It was the light blue, almost piercing eyes that particularly did it for her though.

The flat itself was nice, a mix of bohemian-type clutter Justine had picked up here and there, some artwork she had dabbled with on the advice of one of her old sixth form tutors, along with some pretty decent antique furniture the landlord had left. And there was the rather impressive hi-fi system Mark had bought for them, with the two speakers looking like sentries and doubling as plant stands either side of the bay window. Mark and his department had sorted a research grant which covered the basics and she knew Mark spent all his spare money on her and they'd had a pretty good time of it. In fact as she waited for him to arrive, Justine felt a surge of warmth.

Even if it was another snatched night, they always had a good time, whether having a laugh or a philosophical debate it never seemed difficult; and she'd had plenty of that with other dates and lovers. Anyway it would do for now but she wasn't so easily impressed or perhaps satisfied as Mark and she knew she had the looks that clearly could lead to a better lifestyle than a doctorate in social psychology might provide. Although Mark had stuck with it and made a career for himself, maybe four years of Sociology was more than enough for most; and certainly for anyone with her imagination.

Last weekend had been something of a surprise and real eye-opener for her. She'd gone with Mark to one of his old university friend's houses for a reunion party, for the first time as his 'official' partner, even though he was still married to Fiona. The party was at a country cottage that Tom had just bought, outside the village of Ditchling, off the road to Lewes. It was a part of the county Mark had visited many times when he was a growing up in Brighton: there had been family picnics at weekends as well as school outings onto the Downs. The names of the villages around mid-Sussex read like a children's fairy-tale, Plumpton Green, Cowfold, Burgess Hill and Hassocks; and the quaint local pubs always reminded Mark of Sunday afternoon outings with his family. However, it wasn't the location of Tom's cottage but the style and lavishness of it that knocked Justine out: the garden had been rigged out with a marquee and lights around the trees marking the boundary, the makeshift bar was stocked with every sort of aperitif and spirit she could think of, there were upturned barrels each bedecked with small trays of coke, razors and mirrors and bowls of ready rolled joints, speakers were dotted around the chairs and tables. Of course, she realized he'd got it through family money, but for someone only a few years older than her to have this gorgeous country house was certainly head-turning, and the way he effortlessly made them all feel welcome. On top of that, and particularly, there was the way he had looked at her. Justine was happy with Mark but it was nice to get that kind of response from one of his old friends, especially one as classy as Tom, and even if it perhaps had been a little pervy.

Justine had a natural elegance: not over-tall at just over five foot six, she exuded class and fun in equal measure. Her full figure contrasted with the emaciated hippy style look that had been common since the mid-sixties, her henna'd hair shone and her eyes, hinting green, sparkled. Justine knew she was good looking, and she knew men thought so too, but she didn't flaunt it. She just accepted it and dealt with the looks and attention, maybe that was why she had never made any really close friendships with other girls. She was quite well liked and had acquaintances for sure, but she'd always felt an undercurrent of envy. Anyway, they were mainly stuck up snobs with no class or just basically dull. For sure, she was ambitious and knew she was a lot smarter than many of those she had graduated with, but she wasn't as materialistic, or even money-grabbing, as Mark had on occasion managed to make her feel. She had been flattered with the attention Mark had given her, the time he spent explaining what she had or hadn't done in the various and tedious theory essays he'd been her tutor for. She remembered the first time he'd asked her to go for a coffee with him; it was during her final term as an undergraduate over a year ago, how that had led to lunchtime meetings and drinks. It had all been quite innocent and almost quaint, the way he'd pursued her under the veil of his tutoring role, how on a couple of occasions he'd even found a flimsy excuse to call round to the house she was sharing in her final year. That had been during her last few weeks there. She had been pleased that the apartment he'd helped her get after graduating was only a stone's throw away from that shared student house. It had amused her, too, how he'd finally taken the plunge at the end of year do and asked her to go for a drive with him. No doubt he'd thought his sports car would win her over.

That final year had been good, and especially the last few weeks; she liked the looks she got from her fellow students when she was seen with Mark, she liked the money he spent on her and, fair enough, his car was pretty flash. On one level things were still good, but once she'd started her postgrad course and moved into the apartment Justine had gradually come to realize that they both had different agendas and paths. She knew she wanted something more and that even if she couldn't do better, however that might be measured, she wanted to do something different. Justine certainly didn't feel she was or ever would be a sociologist, whatever that might entail. Becoming an academic held no great attraction for her, it was certainly not a goal that she cherished. The last few months spending time with Mark and on a few occasions recently with one or other of his colleagues as well had put a different gloss on university life and academia. They still had fun but she could see Mark was becoming too obsessed and desperate really; she knew they were never going to have the future he'd been talking about but couldn't seem to get around to dealing with it or even raising it with him. It was easy enough to rationalize too, after all he was having a good time with her, she made sure they had good sex and plenty of it, and he was a good deal older than her so surely he should be able to behave that way and deal with things when they ran their course. And, of course, he was still married, for all his talk; yes, she had no need to feel obliged. On balance, it was easier to just enjoy things as they were for the time being and doubtless it would all fall into place. That rationalization and approach even had a nice, post-hippy kind of feeling. She was aware that maybe her attitude was all a little tongue in cheek, after all she'd never considered herself some sort of free-spirited, hippy chick, a dreadful label and description that surely no right-minded woman could answer to. She was only just 23 and things had worked out so far, so why not take it as it comes and deal with Mark and any fall-out at the right time?

**

Mark had completed his fourth year at the university and Justine hadn't been the first time he'd taken some advantage of the perks offered as a consequence of easily impressed female undergraduates, or for that matter presumably male ones too, looking to experiment with new lifestyles and new drugs. It wasn't that he felt he'd grown up but he knew that last year's departmental end of year party had signalled some sort of turning point for him. After all, he had taken the trouble to persuade Justine to stay on and take the new postgraduate course that his department had just had validated, so he'd forced his own hand; and now, in spite of the fact it was going well out of any comfort zone and was likely to change his life for ever, he felt kind of excited and drawn to the whole idea. He parked alongside the railings of the gardens separating Devonshire Place and Chapel Street, found the bell for the fourth apartment of number 32. He'd visited once or twice a week since he'd paid the deposit and Justine had signed a year's lease on the apartment. It had been an odd departmental meeting when the decisions were made as to which of their graduates deserved the few grants they had for supervising research students. Mark hadn't wanted to make it too obvious and had canvassed support from Sandra and a couple of the others who weren't themselves over-keen on having to supervise eager young postgraduates for the next three years, and who seemed more than happy for him to offer. Anyway he'd manoeuvred it so that he was allocated Justine and one other plus a decent number of hours as well. Postgraduate supervision was for him an easy way of filling his timetable and impressing everyone that he was at the cutting edge of the discipline. While it might not be the pinnacle of academic achievement, supervising doctoral students was pretty easy work if you could get it, to paraphrase the sentiments of one of his previous tutors.

He'd got to love this part of Brighton too, even though he'd hardly noticed it in his boyhood years in his family home. He liked the feeling it evoked, of a fading grandeur with the great town houses largely either apartments or occasionally guesthouses; and he felt the nature of the area changing from what had presumably been genteel middle class to a mix of tourism and bohemia – Brighton was a cool place and with the university expanding and a nicely established underground youth culture continuing on from the 1960s it seemed a good place to be. He knew it couldn't stay the same for him and he would have to move on with his and Justine's lives; and he knew he'd need to keep his self-belief strong, even if it might turn out misplaced. Meanwhile he might as well face it, things weren't that bad when he looked back. It had been a pretty cool year, some great times with Justine, and the subterfuge was really quite exhilarating and hadn't been too hard to manage either. Sure, he had cut himself off a little from his mates and let his marriage drift, but then when he thought about it so had Fiona. Justine was something else and she was bloody gorgeous.

Of course there had been some fallout with his colleagues over his involvement with Justine – and particularly with the part-time tutoring he'd arranged for her; no overt hostility, just some thinly-disguised disapproval from one or two. His lack of interest in any of the departmental social do's or even internal wrangling had been noticed by a few of them as well. Before Justine, Mark had always been up for a gossip and debate and had seemed to his colleagues, and, well, probably actually had been, committed to academia and the developing role of Sociology. He'd liked to think that he was even seen as something of a rising star. Sandra had been the most troublesome; he hadn't realized how much she'd come to rely on their supposedly special relationship. When he'd arrived as a new lecturer four years back now, at the start of the 1970 academic year, he had soon established himself as Mr Sociable, and had since become the main party and drinking organiser in the department – a role he had enjoyed but which didn't really fit in with where he'd moved to over the last few months.

Last year's departmental party played back briefly as he waited for Justine to answer, which involved her coming down the stairs now that the intercom had finally died. Although the party had been much the same as the previous few years this time Mark had felt a sort of detachment that he couldn't quite put his finger on. It wasn't the drink or drugs; he'd always had a pretty strong degree of self-control and apart from a few days when he'd been a student at Kent he'd never lost his grip as he'd seen a few of his friends do. He remembered quite clearly feeling that the next year would be different and that premonition was beginning to prove correct. He'd been sitting at the edge of the square with Sandra, his boss, Mike, and a few other Faculty staff. There was a local student band playing some West Coast-inspired and endless jam; it wasn't that different from the campus party at Kent in 1969 after his own graduation. Maybe he just hadn't grown up but that had been when, with his upper second class degree, gained with a minimum of effort or attendance, and having had a good relationship and time with some of the younger members of the new Sociology department, he'd decided the best way to avoid growing up any more was to inveigle his way into university teaching. In fact, looking back it might seem as if it had all been supremely well planned – the department there had been keen to support him following their new Master's course and were happy to let him have a few hours tutoring on the increasingly popular Sociology courses to lighten their hours.

The job at Sussex had come up a year after he'd graduated and the department at Kent had provided glowing references – helped by his promise to continue supplying them with the drugs a couple of them felt they needed to remain sufficiently cool in their students' eyes at least. Anyway, there were still relatively few Sociology postgraduates to choose from – and having a few hours' teaching experience on his CV was seen as a godsend; and it didn't do any harm that his supervisor at Kent and early mentor, Jon, had been a friend of Mike's at Sussex. It amazed him that it never struck supposedly intelligent, right-on people as odd that they all spent hours lecturing, writing and debating about inequality, class and the evils of privilege but had no apparent problem putting themselves and their friends first. Nonetheless, the networking among the lecturers in the burgeoning Sociology departments of the period had worked pretty smoothly for him and a good few of his postgraduate contemporaries too. Get a foot in the door and sure enough the jobs came along.

***

The four years in Sussex had gone quite well and Mark had become pretty well regarded and established. He had always had a good rapport with the students, and because he wasn't unwilling to take on extra teaching, he was deemed a good colleague; even by Dr Webb who couldn't believe some of the courses the younger staff had managed to get approved. The department he'd joined just after completing his MA in the summer of 1970 was overwhelmingly young and undeniably trendy; looking back it was almost appallingly so but it had been fun and they were basically a pretty decent group to work with. Only two of the nine full-time lecturers were clearly over 40 and had been there from the opening of the university in the early 1960s, initially as itinerant social scientists before the setting up of separate Sociology and Politics departments in most of the new universities of the time. While the sociologists appointed since then and before Mark spent a lot of the coffee time, common room breaks and early evening drinking sessions taking the piss out of Dr Webb and Ms Carey and their lack of interest in the ethnographic case study research that was all the rage with the new sociology and deviancy groups, Mark made a point of getting to know them too and of being interested in their work as well. He had always felt there would be some benefit from spreading his charm; even as a student, and really even at school, he had made a point of making friends with the less popular kids and students, the ones who didn't want to play football or get stoned, depending on the time or context. Maybe it was a sort of charitable impulse, but he certainly kind of liked being one of the cool ones, but the type who was actually so cool that he didn't mind being seen with the uncool. Thinking of it he wondered why; maybe some sort of safety net or psychological need to be liked by as many people as possible. Anyhow, it extended to his colleagues in the department too. He'd spend a good few hours sitting in Dr Webb's study (he couldn't quite get used to calling him Ernest) and not just feigning interest, but actually trying to understand the sampling and chi-squaring and general number-crunching – and even offering to help with the tutorials on quantitative methods that the rest of the department and most of the students hated in just about equal measure.

Most of the time Mark actually liked the students, he enjoyed having a drink at lunchtime with them and he enjoyed being invited to the odd party. He'd even taken to buying a bit of dope and the odd package of coke from a couple of his third years, as it was easier than going over to his previous contacts in Kent. And allowing the odd joint in his tutorials had ensured his option at year 3 was always oversubscribed. Come to think of it, he really quite liked his role and status and it didn't seem difficult to do enough to fit in and even to get on – he'd go to at least one conference a term, turn up and ask a sensible question at the departmental research seminars and make sure his papers got published. Given that there were so few books and journals covering the sociology of culture that wasn't much of an issue either. His English was fine and Mike, his boss, had put him in touch with his own publishing agent, so his research profile was already looking strong. It had helped that Mark had always enjoyed reading and acquiring books, so much so that his office was pretty fast becoming a library and not just with social science texts. He remembered how his mum had given him a copy of Dostoyevsky's *The Idiot* when he was fourteen, and since then he'd read most of the classics, Russian, French – Hugo, Balzac, Zola – and lots of contemporary hip American stuff, the trendy 'beat' generation, but also the great earlier twentieth-century novels of Scott Fitzgerald, Steinbeck, Faulkner and Dos Passos. When he started his BA Sociology degree at university in late 1966 he had cultivated an image of a widely-read bibliophile, which had added a balance to the usual drinking and drug-taking and had been a great help in impressing girls. Sitting in his study bedroom or on the easy chairs in the communal kitchen-cum-lounge with a glass of wine or Southern Comfort while reading Steinbeck or Kerouac seemed a pretty sure-fire way of ensuring a steady supply of fellow students to share his nights with.

The reminiscences were really most enjoyable and he felt a satisfied glow. Since then, and after pairing off with Fiona during his final term as a student, there had been the odd dalliance but overall he had been pretty loyal to Fiona, and anyway he was pretty sure it had been reciprocal; the fact that neither of them questioned the other's occasional absences or whereabouts had convinced him of that. And after all it reflected the period, it wasn't that long after the sixties – he knew she hadn't minded his regular trips to conferences, and she must have a pretty shrewd idea of what went on at them. Her lack of concern for his movements had become noticeably more obvious after they had bumped into a previous boyfriend of hers in a shop he had leased in the Lanes soon after they'd moved to Brighton. Mark had wondered at the time whether it was perhaps not a completely chance meeting. James had been at Brighton College, oddly named for a well-regarded public school, while Fiona was at nearby Roedean; and Brighton College boys were the only ones let anywhere near Roedean girls. After they had married, he'd helped Fiona decorate in 'period style' the house her parents had provided just down the road from them in Ovingdean.

Mark had only been 23 and Fiona 21 when they'd got married, just after he'd completed his MA and been offered his first job in the fledgling Sociology department at Sussex and after she'd graduated with her BA. Although Mark had seen her around the campus in Canterbury and knew her as one of the girls from the floor above, they'd only got together the Easter beforehand and had a pretty good time finishing their courses together. Mark had loved her posh accent and obviously upper class manners. They'd spent a couple of weekends that summer at her parents' quite grand house in Rottingdean and he'd been happy enough when Fiona's dad, Gordon, had said he'd buy them a house near theirs if they got married. Having retired from running his own estate agent's business in London a few years ago, Gordon was absolutely convinced of the value of and sense in buying property and as Fiona was his only child, it was perhaps not such a surprising gesture. Mark supposed Gordon was of that mindset and generation that wasn't too happy about sex before marriage; and anyway, why not take advantage of some family money? He was going to be working nearby and it'd save some rent. After all, they might as well reap the benefit of Fiona's family's wealth, maybe it hadn't been the most 'right on' of attitudes but it was kind of re-distributing wealth from a rich old capitalist to someone who'd use it better; one way of looking at it, he rationalized. The only thing Mark had insisted on was a very low-key wedding, and as Fiona had agreed to that it had all been sorted in a few weeks that summer.

Fiona had been taken with what she assumed was Mark's sensitivity; she was studying literature and liked the fact he'd read most of the course texts she was supposed to study. And she wanted to have a good time before leaving the student lifestyle. Her parents had made it clear they expected her to come back home after it and she hadn't any particular plans otherwise. Fiona had quite quickly come to realize that even though they had some good times together and had both agreed that getting married was what they wanted, Mark was never going to be her soulmate. He wasn't into art and poetry in the way that she was. Within a few weeks of their marriage she was pretty sure that it hadn't been the right decision; it might turn out fine, but if it didn't she realized she wasn't too bothered either. In point of fact, that realization really helped her: why not keep up the façade for a while? Her parents would always be on her side whatever she decided to do. Anyway, she knew she held the aces, Mark would be more tied to her than the other way around. Meanwhile she had heard from an old school friend that James, the only one of her previous boyfriends she'd ever really felt close to, was opening a shop in the Lanes and had even asked after her. It wasn't that Fiona had no feelings for Mark, and she knew he cared for her, it just wasn't all she wanted; and she knew Mark probably felt the same.

***

Yes, that July night and end of year party had been a key moment, even if at the time it had just seemed the usual sort of scenario. It had been another lovely evening and the university square looked alive. Sandra had been plying him and Mike with drinks – and they'd been talking about the new candidates and how they might help develop the department, but he'd been happy to leave her and Mike to decide who to shortlist. That was all always pretty informal anyway – the Sociology world was a small one – previous postgraduate students who'd taken the odd tutorial and whose faces fitted. He'd suggested they go and congratulate the new graduates and mingle a little.

However, and in retrospect, it had been different and it had led to this and to Devonshire Place and Justine. It had really all come back to him in a brief moment as he waited for the door of flat 32D to open. That party had been the time he'd decided he wanted more than a fling. It had been time for him to benefit from the perks of three years of trying to impress students that Marx, Durkheim and Weber were relevant and even inspiring. It wasn't that it had worn him out. He'd established a pleasant enough niche running the sociology of culture option for final year students and now supervising a couple of postgraduate students too. Even though his course had been little more than an opportunity for his students, and being honest for him too, to show off just how in tune and hip they were, it had attracted lots of takers; and it had certainly been a bit of a challenge to and change from the social administration and policy options on offer. More to the point, Justine and a couple of her mates had opted for it in their final year. Some of the sessions had carried over into the university bar – he remembered one evening discussing the merits of Aztec culture and another on the relationship between love and sex in the writing, or perhaps more accurately ramblings, of the Marquis de Sade. He'd left a few of them to it but knew he'd ignited a spark of interest from Justine that he'd be able to work on.

***

A couple of days before that party Sandra had made a point of asking him to make sure he came by himself and he'd not really needed to explain to Fiona that it was the usual departmental do and he'd be late. He remembered guessing that 'Antique James' was doubtless in her mind anyway. Sandra had been good to him when he was new to the job four years ago – she'd been there a couple of years longer and had been appointed his mentor. She'd taken the role beyond helping him to plan lectures and mark assignments and he hadn't complained. Even though he reckoned that she was less than ten years older than him it had been his 'The Graduate' moment and since then they'd mixed working together with a weekly drink and pretty decent afternoon sex. Sandra was a change from the girls he'd been with at university, she was big and colourful and while she was outgoing and loud in public and liked a good drink or two, she was quite subservient and even submissive in bed. Although she ran the obligatory feminist sociology option he liked the way she certainly didn't fit the stereotype. At first it had bothered him that Sandra had insisted they keep the liaison a secret from their colleagues, but now he was extremely grateful that she had. She was good company and he knew he wouldn't be able to avoid feeling his increasingly obvious feelings for Justine would be seen as something of a betrayal; particularly as her contacts and advice had helped him establish a place in the growing social science scene and a reputation of sorts. The academic life both appealed to him and repulsed him: some days it seemed a great place to be and even exciting in its own way, other times it really was a self-indulgent charade. Some of his colleagues both here and on the circuit were undeniably pretty bright and writing some quite impressive texts, but they certainly weren't changing any worlds except their own. Basically academics were a pretty privileged lot and aside from a few most of the others didn't even strike him as intelligent. It amazed him how they managed to spend their time in a constant moan about how stressed and hard worked they were – as if a deadline for a paper, as they grandly called them, that might consist of a few pages of analysis and perhaps a creative sentence or two, was a matter of any great import. It all depended on your comparables really, and the newer staff would always feel hard done by in relation to the various and oddly titled senior managers – the pro-vice chancellors and deans who were living off reputations gained from some fairly basic research and writing done years ago and regurgitated in a few key places.

When he had turned up for the do itself and after a couple of drinks, Sandra had slipped her hand through his and suggested they go across the square to her office. It was odd that he recalled thinking that surely she could sense that he felt different and that it wasn't going to go any further. He'd had to manoeuvre an escape and thank goodness Mike was there and agreed with him that they should make an effort to mingle. Mark had taken the lead and commented:

'After all, the results have been great and we shouldn't be standoffish.'

It wasn't the most elegant of ploys but he'd seen Dr Webb and Stephanie the departmental administrator hove into view. He knew the group of year 3's he'd marked over-generously would be pleased to see him and he knew there was a good chance there'd be plenty of coke and dope later; and Sandra had her sociology of gender group to congratulate. It was a little odd that he worried more about what Sandra would think and how she'd react, rather than his wife; no doubt even a part-time feminist would interpret it as being used, and anyway Fiona bumping into James had taken some of the guilt and hassle away as well. Sandra knew he spent a lot of time talking to and ogling over Justine but then he'd done that a good bit over the years so presumably she hadn't seen this as any different, or as signalling the end of a relationship which Mark conveniently assumed had been good for her, casual but fun enough, proving she still had it even though she was a fair bit older than him.

**

Back to the present, he wasn't certain why he felt a little anxious about tonight, he always looked forward to time with Justine but there was a sense of desperation and need creeping up on him. Sure, they would no doubt have a good time and get stoned, but he knew it wasn't the promise of that which attracted him but more the chance of some quality time together.

All the recent history had played back in his mind in little more than the few minutes he had taken to drive to the flat and wait for Justine to answer the door. The images and memories continued to run across his mind. Justine had sort of crept up on him: the number of lectures he'd given and tutorials he'd supervised when she had gradually shown more and more of her cleavage and figure had had its effect. She always made an entrance, whether to a class or just to the common room at coffee time; or perhaps it was only he who noticed, but he doubted it. She probably had no idea and he'd probably imagined it but he had sensed this was a key moment and event; and that while nothing might change straightaway if the opportunity, and opportunity for what was absolutely unclear to him, was not considered and acted on, then nothing would change at all. And thinking back it wasn't that he was dissatisfied or searching – he actually had quite liked the way things were and wasn't the sort of person to dwell on might be's. Yes, it just had to happen then and he surprised himself that he could remember the occasion and the details with almost perfect recall; and also why he was thinking that now, and how he had not done so for most of the previous twelve months. Maybe it was a nod to his brief flirting with science fiction writing, when Bradbury, Heinlein and even Asimov and Vonnegut had seemed to knock over conventional constraints, but since then, perhaps as some sort of re-establishing of structures, he liked to locate events in a time frame. He needed to, or liked to at least, see how one event, how one awareness linked with and led to the next.

The Faculty of Social Sciences had almost 1,500 students, including the 300 or so in his department, and there had been a pretty good turnout that July evening last year, groups of staff and students had spread out to the park beyond the main campus; as well as the incense there was the distinct smell of pot. Even the political groups with their right-on slogans and missionary zeal weren't averse to getting stoned. It was like a rite of passage from the hopes and dreams of making things better, to post-graduate training courses to be social workers, teachers or civil servants; but with the perhaps naïve optimism that they might be able to 'change things from within'. That was the way of things and Mark couldn't really take the high ground, he'd been earning a good salary filling their heads with what in all likelihood would be of little use to them or their worlds. Justine was sitting on a bench next to the Socialist Worker stall, being managed by two of his third year group; to think he'd developed a sociology of culture course for them. He wandered across the square and pulled up a chair between Justine and a makeshift table stacked with flyers, worthy-looking pamphlets and other calls to action.

'Hi Justine, so what's your plans for next year?'

Unless he'd completely misread the signals and looks when he gave back the final essays a few weeks before the end of year exams and then graduation, he assumed Justine would be pleased to see him and surely wouldn't mind a break from the right-on brigade. They'd been discussing the need for students to support the TUC's protests over government pay restraint and price rise policies. She and a couple of other final year students had been making arrangements to go and help train for picket line duty, should that be needed later in the summer; and presumably before they left for whatever future careers they had planned. That wasn't the way Mark had it planned out though, he'd been giving things some thought and had decided he would do his best to persuade her to stay on at Sussex and then see how things panned out.

'You'd be perfect for the new Master's in Social and Cultural Theory and there are bursaries and grants I could look into to cover the fees and more.'

He managed to manoeuvre her away and got the distinct impression she was thinking she could do with a break from the hairies and beardies. Strange that his distinct impressions were usually the reflection of what he actually wanted to be the case – probably taking the self-fulfilling prophecy too far, but it was always a topic his students grasped pretty comfortably. There'd be time for her to be a radical later, or better just to forget about it anyway, and he guessed she would be pretty keen to get on and live a little. Really, that was all beside the point: he wanted to get her and wasn't without practice or success in getting his own way. After all there had to be some side applications and benefits of learning how to keep a hundred-plus students amused and on-message for an hour or so three times a week. He'd suggested a walk around the campus park and lake and then perhaps a drive down to the village pub.

***

Although he had been oddly nervous and hadn't made his usual, and come to think of it predatory and hackneyed, move, it had been a nice almost-first date, he reminisced. Justine had rolled a couple of joints and even though it wasn't really his thing, Mark had pretended to be keen. It wasn't that Mark was against drugs: he'd made a fair extra living when at university in Kent from buying in bulk, and dealing had helped him get well known and liked by the trendier and younger staff there and, indirectly, had no doubt helped him get his current position. He just didn't like it any more than a decent beer or drop of Southern Comfort or Bourbon. Driving around in the Morgan had helped and after a few days out later that summer, and once they'd got to know each other, things had been pretty good.

The first time he'd actually asked her out and they had spent some time together he had finally acted out of role, as the social psychologists would put it. He'd parked at the top of Moulscombe Park and they'd found a spot to sit and take in the late summer view over Brighton in one direction and the Downs the other way. Justine hadn't resisted when he pulled her over to him. It was a little bizarre thinking back but the fact she didn't resist had actually thrown him. It wasn't the first time he'd seduced, that was really the only word, a student but this had felt different. He'd moved his hand down from her breasts and into her tight jeans and the moment he felt her mound and her wet lips he just hoped she wouldn't do the same to him – not just yet anyway, he knew he was too excited. But she hadn't waited, she'd unzipped his jeans and as soon as she touched him he'd been unable to stop himself. It ranked amongst the most embarrassing moment of his life, but that was water under the bridge. He liked the way she'd been so matter of fact; and she'd let him take her out a couple of days later and make up for it. After that it had been easy and different and Justine had seemed more than satisfied. Mark realized he had never really bothered that much about his partner's experience before Justine. In fact, he remembered being surprised when one had asked him to give her cunnilingus, the definition of which he'd had to look up in his Chambers Dictionary later. With Justine, he made sure she got as much pleasure as he did.

In the period after the final exams and end of year party and before her graduation, Mark had helped Justine apply for the course and get the grant for fees and living costs. There had been the usual rumours that support for postgraduates was not going to last but at the time there was still plenty of Social Science Research Council monies around – and only a smallish number of half-baked research proposals to distribute them to. In fact, when his colleagues had agreed to fund a study of the effects of western culture on the lifestyle of native females in North West Botswana and then a post-structural critique of matriarchal domination he'd been pretty confident that her planned research into new religious movements and their relationship to popular culture would get the go-ahead.

They'd looked around Brighton for a flat for her and this one, on one of the elegant squares not far off the top promenade and up towards Kemp Town, had been ideal. Perhaps surprisingly it hadn't caused as much hassle with Fiona as he had expected, she hadn't seemed over-bothered about him claiming to be snowed under at work and having to attend seminars and conferences on a more regular basis than ever before. She had even encouraged him to spend as much time at work as he needed – maybe she had her own secrets, and when he came to think of it then so much the better if she had.

***

Since then he'd enjoyed the double life – in fact it seemed easier than trying too hard with too many different students. He'd been paying for all the extras, the outings and trips away and gigs and drinks and even her drugs. And the work at university was becoming easy enough. He'd always found that part easy – he liked the buzz from lecturing and teaching and he'd always tried to show a little humility and humanity, and simply that he cared about the students' views. It really wasn't difficult to be popular and even respected if you made the effort – don't be patronizing, don't show off too much and demonstrate a dash of enthusiasm at least. It was just about being aware and normal, he couldn't understand how some of his colleagues didn't seem able to communicate – everyone had experienced good and bad teachers themselves, it was just a matter of doing what you felt had worked, along with a little empathy. When Mark was first offered a couple of hours part-time tutoring, he'd promised himself that he would never forget how he'd felt in similar sessions when he started out at university as an 18 year-old, and it had worked for him since then.

The thing was that after a year on the taught Master's programme that served as preparation for the research side of the course, Justine was beginning to get bored; even he had to admit that the course itself was pretty dull, even pointless. For reasons of convenience and economies of scale, the department had decided to run generic courses on social research and social theories in the first term which had involved a mish-mash of talks on different examples of social science research and theory; and even if the options after that had gone better, the dye had been cast. Justine had too much going for her to settle into the academic world.

More to the point, Justine was becoming an even more classy-looking woman: they were both used to the looks they (and mainly she) got whenever they were out and about. He knew she wouldn't be satisfied with the still slightly cloak-and-dagger existence indefinitely. And she would clearly have to be looked after in a manner which it was obvious she could get from any number of the lecherous and generally irritatingly rich mates of his who they partied and drunk with from time to time, most recently at Tom's the week before. Given Fiona's apparent lack of interest in Mark's spending more and more time supposedly at work, he had got round to introducing Justine to some of his friends. He liked showing her off, he liked the effect she had and he liked how it reflected on him too. Most of the people he'd knocked around with at university had somehow managed to do better than him – albeit with the help of their families. When he'd arrived at Kent after a year doing slightly more interesting A levels than he'd followed at school at the local tech college, he'd mainly hung out with ex-public school kids who'd never been too bothered about running up overdrafts and some debts, confident they'd be bailed out after a decent amount of grovelling. It wasn't just about the background and privilege though, it was also the confidence, verging on arrogance, that they had had drummed into them and that had become almost second nature. Then, to be fair, on top of that there was the relative ease with which a brain and a modicum of energy managed to open up lots of ways of making pretty easy money in the early 1970s. It was, he knew, inevitable that Justine would want the best, she hadn't come from a rich background but she knew how to enjoy herself, she didn't care too much about being sensible and she knew the effect she had on men. Since the early summer and since Justine's enthusiasm for social theory and methods was clearly dwindling. Mark had been developing a plan, he knew he had to keep it to himself, but somehow had also been managing to keep it, or perhaps the implications of it, from himself too. Maybe it was just too off the wall, it would definitely involve a bizarre change of lifestyle, which probably explained why it was being stored in the recesses of his mind. Then again, perhaps it reflected the fact that his general reading had changed from juggling with the string-of-consciousness offerings of American beat writers and ex-hippies to histories of crime and murder and their detection.

He couldn't accept that this development had happened through some sort of osmosis, developing almost accidently. Surely it was all linked and pointing out a new direction for him. He'd had little time for the craze some of his contemporaries at university had had for reading Tarot cards and messing around with the I Ching but perhaps fate, predestination or however it was cloaked wasn't all so misplaced after all.

As the sea breeze funnelled up from the Channel to the square, and guests were parking and locating their venues for a weekend by the sea in one or other of the elegant, four-storey houses which had been turned into B and B's and guest houses rather than flats, Mark wondered why he'd never taken the time to analyse how and why things had come to this. He watched a young family arrive in a new Mark II Cortina which the father was parking with obsessive caution, checking the width of the road between the outside driver's door and the railings surrounding the shared garden, and then supervising the emptying of the beach apparel from the boot. Further down, a well-dressed, silver-haired man in his fifties with a bright red Triumph Spitfire, sashayed round it to give a hand to a much younger blonde lady, a girlfriend or weekend accomplice. He felt he could be or become a player in either of those scenarios, wondering what way would it all pan out – family man or playboy, to put it crudely.

In a way he wasn't surprised that Sandra had been a problem. She had caught him at lunchtime the day after the staff-student end of year party that he'd just been playing back to himself on the drive to the flat. At the time it had seemed kind of threatening when she sat next to him in the common room and commented:

'She may be pretty but you know we're good together and good for each other.'

Mark had put it out of his mind, he liked Sandra and they'd had some nice afternoons together and she was good fun and even if it did seem shallow he assumed they both accepted that, but there were other things he wanted. He knew that he needed to stay with Fiona for the time being at least, if for no other reason than her family's position and the potential access to money, and even more so now he needed to work out how to keep going, or really begin, some sort of semi-glamorous lifestyle for Justine. Sandra hadn't minded his other dalliances but then they'd never got in the way, but she'd obviously sensed things would be different this time. Since the day after that party, Mark had tried to be as friendly and charming to her as possible but he had engineered a series of excuses to avoid any more afternoons and she knew he had too.

Now, while waiting to see Justine, he realized that for some reason over the few months they'd been sort of together, he had developed a stronger loyalty to her than he ever had to Fiona, let alone Sandra. Maybe it was because he couldn't stand the idea of Justine being with anyone else; and he was beginning to feel the same about himself. He'd started off with a quite liberal, or what passed as liberated, approach to Justine, and had even pretended to be interested in finding her a long-term partner, but that hadn't lasted more than a few weeks. There had been a vicarious kind of pleasure from feigning an interest in Justine's descriptions of men she'd met up with and men she'd gone to bed with too. As long as they hadn't met her demands that had been fine, but it could only ever have been a game and a short-lived one. Sure, he'd been quite turned on when she described one encounter when, after a night of showing off, the guy couldn't get hard; or the time she'd gone back to a hotel with a couple of supposed businessmen, teased them to take their clothes off and done a runner before they'd twigged. Thing was, he might only hear of the occasions and ones she wanted him to. Jealousy may not be the most attractive of traits, and certainly not one he felt comfortable applying to himself, but surely it signified some degree of caring, and that was better than thinking it was just paranoia.

The last few months, and really the whole of the last academic year, had been awkward in the department, Sandra had remained civil but rarely spoke to him; and made a great play of her friendship with Mike – which Mark was more than grateful for. He'd had to watch her, though. A few snide digs about inappropriate staff-student relationships had been made at staff meetings and particularly their end of year review day that year; and he knew Sandra would get support in those points from Anne, their newly appointed feminist colleague, and a perfect example of the genre. Really, it was worrying him to see that the Sociology department was gradually moving towards becoming a feminist, and potentially lesbian, enclave. Another reason to get out.

And now here she was, his mistress, or maybe paramour –
even if both the terms reminded him of the French literature
that he'd tried to explain to the culture group was without doubt
far more insightful as well as just more readable compared to
the completely unstructured jumble that Ginsberg, Burroughs
and their cronies, even Kerouac, seemed to think of as literature
or culture. Thank goodness he'd been touched by the literature
A level he'd taken in his sixth form at grammar school. It had
been an all-boys school and literature hadn't been a popular
choice amongst his peers, but he had loved reading and
deconstructing Golding's *Lord of the Flies* and Steinbeck's *Of
Mice and Men*, as well as Chaucer and Shakespeare; and his
trendy English teacher, Mr Wills, who broke convention with
his sweater and cords rather than a jacket and tie, had
introduced him to Aldous Huxley too. He still felt that even
after the last few years of immersing himself in the brave new
world of sociology, those works continued to have more to say
and more to teach than the beat poetry, feminist mystique and
stream of consciousness offerings populating the burgeoning
new and old bookshops appearing off Queens Road and just up
the road here in hip Kemp Town.

***

It seemed to Mark that he'd reviewed his entire recent life in
the few minutes he'd taken to park and ring the bell. Justine
turned the lock and opened the communal door to number 32.
She looked as great as ever; she could look classy as well as
hip, and while mostly it was jeans and slightly see-through
cheesecloth tops, tonight she was wearing a tight fitting and
short dress that showed off her great figure. This was one of the
things that for Mark set her apart – her confidence in her
appearance and body; and her willingness to stand out from the

ubiquitous flowery hippy look that again seemed to have taken over Brighton so far this summer. They'd even had a few themed dates, once when she'd got hold of a sort of flapper-inspired twenties dress and he'd worn a big lapelled gangster-style suit.

Mark had planned this particular night as an anniversary date and had booked a table at a little restaurant off the Lanes. There were a couple of local bands playing at the King and Queens later and he'd brought a little coke from a second year student, Greg, as a sort of surprise and attempt to impress. It worried him that he was feeling under a bit of pressure to impress Justine and had had to spend a few days asking around the hipper-looking undergraduates who were still hanging around the campus in order to score this little treat. Maybe it was just they both knew things couldn't go on as they had been indefinitely; after all, the actual teaching on the Master's was just about finished and Justine had really just been doing enough to get by. It was obvious, and understandable really, that she wasn't over-enthused about going on to the PhD research stage; and he was beginning to think academic life for the next three decades might not be living the dream either.

He followed her up the stairs: 'I'm a lucky guy, and you know it won't be like this forever.'

What he really needed though was some reassurance from Justine rather than from himself. She smiled and gave him a quick kiss:

'Come on let's get going, it's too nice to stay here and I'm lucky too.'

Yes maybe all was fine, but he couldn't get a comment that he had overheard from last weekend out of his head; it had been his old room-mate Tom or one of that crowd, joking with her that she surely didn't just want to be 'a dull academic or conference groupie'.

It was probably all in his mind, he was confident enough in his charm and ability and Justine hadn't been complaining, but slightly better than comfy wouldn't do for ever. The concerns had been brought to something of a head when he recalled another conversation he'd overheard from the other evening when they were at Tom's house-warming, a few miles up the road in mid-Sussex. Mark and Justine had spent that weekend with Tom and a few other of his old university crowd plus assorted and trendy others. He knew some of the talk had got to Justine and in particular it was a couple of remarks here and there that had been playing around since then. It wasn't just that, he'd seen some body language that he'd prefer to forget. He had to admit it was a bloody gorgeous place, a thatched cottage in close to an acre's ground, with an outdoor pool and a couple of barns Tom's parents were paying for him to convert for holiday lets and then leaving to him to manage. It was in a beautiful unspoilt part of the South Downs. Tom had made some money himself with a little buying and selling of drugs, but it hadn't really been necessary as he knew his parents were always going to set him up in the property business. Mark and Tom had been inseparable for a couple of years at university; they'd lived the hip student life together and shared a few girls and a lot of drugs. They'd been the best of mates, soul brothers they'd thought, so much so that he recalled that a couple of girls they'd got to know had even assumed they must have been gay.

It wasn't just Tom; the rest of his class of 1970 had somehow managed to do pretty well for themselves by the look of things. His Morgan was usually a talking point but it hadn't looked that special as he'd pulled up the driveway next to the Porsches, Mercs and MGs. Martin had set up a record store and mail order service that had tapped into the trend to buy LPs rather than singles and to go beyond what was promoted in the *New Musical Express*. He had even managed to wheedle his way into the good books of a couple of emerging, and pretty boring, blues bands and certainly had access to tickets for gigs all over the place. Even more unbelievably, Stewart had used a small loan from his aunt to buy into what was now becoming the hippest night club south of the Thames, the Craw Daddy Club in Richmond, and had already hosted bands from the West Coast, as well as a number of the new English blues bands. Most of the others Mark only knew second hand. They'd spent the Saturday night sitting around the pool and gazebo in Tom's garden and Justine had had a great time. Although there were a few girlfriends and random singles, Justine had been the centre of most attention and had enjoyed playing up to it. Martin and Stewart had embroiled her in a debate as to the merits of Peruvian as opposed to Colombian coke, with plenty of sampling. He could hardly blame Justine for having a good time but the obviousness of the way most of the males, irrespective of whoever of the various hippy type chicks were draped over them, couldn't take their eyes of her whenever she went for a drink or stroll round the grounds had been verging on the ridiculous. Mark knew Tom from their university days together and he knew he wouldn't trust him where women were concerned; he'd already noted that Tom hadn't spent much of the evening with his own girlfriend Jenny, who to be fair didn't seem over-bothered about that either.

Of course they were still pretty close as a group – Mark had spent a couple of summers travelling with Tom, Martin and Stewart, and had spent the last one of their university days, the summer of '69, mainly in the small, slowly-developing village of Malia, on the north coast of Crete, helping run a bar for the travellers and American GIs stationed up the road. There was, or had been anyway, an unwritten code that put themselves and their friendship first – after one particularly heavy night they'd even pledged never to let any woman come between them. He'd stayed at most of their family homes, as well as at Greek Paul's in Athens – Paul had drifted into their group for a year but had gone back to some pretty high-up government position in Greece after getting his Master's. They'd visited him that summer from Crete but apart from a couple of evenings drinking it was clear from the way he talked about Greek politics and the need to work closely with the army, that he'd moved on and up. So it wasn't that Mark felt awkward or even out of place, but being a comfortable academic was still pretty much under achieving in comparison.

'Still ogling the students then Mark? The summer term was always the best wasn't it?' joked Stewart.

'I could hardly do my jeans up for the whole of the summer most years,' Tom added.

The comments had seemed innocuous but for the first time they had felt kind of patronising. Even reminiscing about their lecturers gave him a feeling of relative stagnation. Martin had joined in.

'Is Webb still harping on about structural Marxism versus structural Functionalism? Don't know how you handle it Mark. And as for bloody women's studies, be OK if it actually was studying women.'

Yes the banter was fun, but Mark felt it was aimed at him a little too much, he didn't see why he should justify things. It just brought home to him that he deserved the same at least as some of those who'd just had it easy. Sure, a few of them were good friends, and why shouldn't they take advantage of their backgrounds, but he was as good as them, and he had the best looking woman there. Maybe it was time to move on and change things, to think through the idea that had been coming and going in his mind and developing for the last few months now. He wanted, he absolutely deserved, the best and that wouldn't be staying where he'd got to.

***

In spite of the supposedly liberated 1960s, the class system still ruled, and quite obviously too; the one or two school friends from his pre-university days and the early girlfriends Mark still kept vaguely in touch with had been astounded by his apparent success in life. In reality, the fact that he'd done just enough to get some qualifications and had talked up his experiences and almost walked into a job where no one seemed to care much what you taught had been easy enough. Nonetheless, it was almost beyond the horizons of his early drinking mates from Sheffield. Here he was, in contrast, in the top few percent, at the top of what passed as the official social class scale, yet even that would never lead to the lifestyle that Justine, or to be fair he himself, expected. Maybe he was reading something into Justine that wasn't there, he just assumed that she would be envious of his friends being better off, even if there was no particular evidence that her philosophy would mirror his.

The real money came from family background but it wasn't just the money: a privileged background seemed almost to breed a certain form of self-belief and drive and just feeling it was one's right. The group Mark had been close to weren't by any means the idle rich, they'd worked hard, but it was being given a leg up to get started in the music business, or the fashion business or the property market or whatever that counted. They certainly weren't stupid, they'd all put the time and effort into their ventures. The key factor was that they had started from a different place; and looking around the garden that night at Tom's and the drinking and drugs and pool, they'd reached somewhere that still stretched way beyond him, unless he looked into the opportunity to utilise the only place close to their starting position within his reach – and that had to be through his wife, Fiona's, family.

Yes, the problem was that these bastards were rolling in it, and if he felt a little outdone it was only natural for Justine to surely feel the same. The evening had ended with some talk of spending next month, early autumn, in Bali but Mark had thought little of it till the next morning when they were preparing to go. He'd noticed Justine chatting to Tom and Jenny, his current missus, but was a little taken aback when she wandered over to the car. 'Come on Mark, they're all off to Bali in a few weeks and they'd love us to come.' Sure, they had been invited, but Mark had not taken it seriously. It would be too difficult to explain to Fiona – they might 'do their own thing' in a manner of speaking but a month or so in a hippy enclave in the Indian Ocean was another matter; and he didn't have that sort of spare money, and they had the apartment in Brighton to keep going. He didn't think those were the sort of explanations likely to excite Justine, so he'd said 'Maybe' as they drove off and back to Brighton. What was happening to him? He felt he'd become even less cool and hip than Tom and that had never occurred to him as a possibility before. He had always been the one who sorted the contacts, who arranged the deals – who took the risks, come to think of it. He was due to spend a bit of time back with Fiona and when he'd explained things to Justine she'd been pretty understanding, but he had a strong inkling that Tom had her number and despite the years of friendship he didn't trust anyone where Justine was concerned.

***

The thing was that Mark needed an additional source of income or capital; and as he'd gradually been considering for a few months now, the in-laws were really the classic if obvious route. For the time being at least, he needed to keep any planning away from Justine. It wasn't going to be a Bonnie and Clyde kind of set-up, and why should she have to get involved when there were plenty of easier routes she could take? If he was going to do this it was his project, even if it was for a long-term future which she'd be sure to appreciate. He had been worried but also kind of excited by thoughts about the perfect crime and about forms of poisoning that had been playing around in his mind for the last few weeks. Although the idea of carrying out anything so basically against all his engrained beliefs about right and wrong had by no means formulated itself into a definite plan, there was no denying it was beginning to creep up on him – subconsciously at the least.

It wasn't any sense of anger or hatred of his conjugal family, it just might be a relatively straightforward way of sorting things reasonably quickly and thereby providing the way of keeping Justine. And maybe it could just be the in-laws; perhaps he and Fiona could come to some kind of arrangement once she had access to the family's wealth. Fiona had been good to him, but she didn't see the need to work for the sake of it, she'd got her degree but her family were more than well off. Indeed they had helped set them up with the house in Ovingdean on the outskirts of town; her dad, Gordon, had certainly been generous enough but always within his somewhat puritanical limits. He doted on his only child and she would never go short, but a social science lecturer at a 'new' university was only just about acceptable; and after all he was probably right to have his suspicions. It was convenient that Fiona was getting more and more into her art work and designing and spending more and more time helping out with James's new art and craft venture in the Lanes.

Jean, his mother-in-law, was another matter, Gordon had made enough with his property speculations to provide a pretty splendid lifestyle for them but it was clear she was bored, with him and their life, and getting even more so. Jean may well have realized she was being hard on her husband, but she still felt short-changed with her lack of excitement. It was also clear that she liked Mark, in part probably because he irritated Gordon, but he liked to think mainly because he was good company.

So that was it, Mark knew Jean was up for being charmed, for some flattery and flirting. It wouldn't be difficult to manoeuvre his way into her favours. She was desperately trying to look less than her 60-plus years but the cigarettes, gin and later than typical childbirth had taken their toll; in fact, she didn't look that healthy at all to Mark. It would be quite a dramatic change of direction for him of course. Mark carried around an image of himself as free and easy but he knew this would need him to focus, and it would involve careful planning and implementing. There would have to be boundaries to observe too, and balance – enough danger to excite her but not to freak her out. Yes it might even be interesting as well as challenging, but he'd been reading up enough on crime to know it would have to be more than a game.

***

Mark put those thoughts aside; for now, he wanted to enjoy some time with Justine. He followed her up to their second-floor apartment: a glimpse of the Channel could be seen from the front window, and a light pink sky helped give the room a warm, late summer, almost autumnal feeling. Justine had lit a couple of candles and the ubiquitous incense sticks before he'd rung the bell. He knew he had to persuade Justine to be patient – he had things to do to sort out their future; but he knew he couldn't risk leaving it too long. He'd seen enough students come and go to realize she was special and worth taking a few more risks than he'd maybe planned to. Over the last few months they'd got into a routine but it had been nice – his job and her postgraduate work gave them plenty of afternoons together. They'd spent many of these wandering down the Lanes and picking up bits and pieces for the flat or just walking along the front before going back to the flat to find out little bits more of and about each other. Somehow she always managed to inspire him yet she'd also managed to become accepted by the other postgraduates and even the feminist sociologists in the department. It was strange, she was quite happy to dress up for him in a schoolgirl's blouse, tie and plaits or in any number of uniforms they'd found in their sorties through the Brighton antique shops, yet she squared this with the dull, dungaree-clad women she spent time with at the university. Only last week she'd pulled his jeans down while they were driving back from a trip to Lewes and worked his cock until he'd come all over the door and window – he hadn't realized just how effective a glue it had been until he'd tried to unwind his window a little later.

The meal had been nicely understated and they were finishing off the bottle of wine before heading down to the King and Queens when he tried to assure her, or more accurately himself, that things would work out:

'I know you don't want things to stay like this for ever, and I'm going to make sure they don't. I need you to be a little patient and we'll extend the lease on Devonshire Place for another six months at least while I spend a bit of time working on a plan I have. I know it might sound a bit cloak and dagger but it's just I'll probably have to spend a little less time with you while I sort out things with Fiona.'

In fact, Justine didn't seem to be too bothered and Mark felt a twinge of anxiety. She reached across the table and grabbed his hand:

'That was a nice meal Mark, thanks, come on let's have that joint and catch the band.'

They walked along Kings Road and the promenade and down onto the pebbles; they'd done this so often over the last few months it was almost a routine too, but this time there seemed to be a difference that he couldn't put his finger on. Over the last few weeks he had been pondering a way forward and had spent a number of days reading about a whole variety of historical crimes and their consequences. Those which had achieved some degree of success, or had at least nearly done so, had typically involved some kind of poisoning and the difficulty or not of tracing it. He'd even spent his recent research leave poring over anthologies of dangerous plants. The old classic was arsenic, and it was still being used on fly papers that most ironmongers and even general stores sold; and barbiturates were easy enough to get hold of, but it was the natural plants and pulses that seemed most plausible. He had discovered that castor beans and kidney beans were pretty dangerous if not prepared properly, that apple pips contained cyanide and that a whole range of pretty heavy-duty and lethal poisons, including antimony, thallium and even arsenic itself, could be picked up at local chemists. It was no wonder chemists and the much more exotically-named apothecaries were such intriguing places.

As the sky darkened and the moon cast a dancing pattern from the sea's horizon right up to where they were standing by the water's edge, he put his arm around Justine; surely she must have an idea of what he was thinking. He knew he'd have to spend some time away from her – it had to be a gradual process and she had to have no idea what he was up to; that was the way he had always thought it should be, there would be no gangster and his moll element to this. After all as he kept reminding himself, Justine had no need to help a would-be serial killer just to have a lifestyle she could achieve easily enough anyway.

Strange how you could know someone so intimately, to want to share a future together and yet have no real idea how they'd react to a carefully planned strategy to give them the future they wanted. If he was concerned that it would be a step too far for her, why not for him? In a way he wasn't surprised to find he was beginning to feel that the next few months would have to see him acting in a sort of semi-automatic way, a kind of moving pavement that would run his life and determine his future.

The anxiety soon wore off after a couple of smokes and a few glasses; it had turned out to be a pretty good night, the music had been good and when they reached the flat after staggering across Victoria Gardens and up Edward Street, Justine had been as up for it and sexy as ever. She'd put on his favourite Grateful Dead album, pulled his jeans down and brought him to a climax in her mouth before they'd got to the bedroom. He didn't like to think of his brain being below his belt, but she hadn't had to spend long getting him hard again before pulling his reddened, now sensitive cock into her and satisfying her own needs. Mark had arranged to stay over for the night as it was the last time he'd get to see her for a few days. When he told Fiona he'd be too drunk to drive home so may as well stay with one of his colleagues in town she hadn't seemed too bothered either.

He remembered being woken up next morning by Justine packing, giving him a quick kiss and dashing to catch the train to London on the way back to Carlisle. As he got his things together and made a cup of tea to waken up, and even though they had had a bloody good last night together before her obligatory end of summer trip back North to see her parents, he couldn't shake off a nagging unease. Surely there was no reason for him to worry. He knew that any false paranoia would be sure to get in the way of things; and after all, he had a few days before she returned to find out if he really had the required nerve or if it was all some sort of deluded fantasy.

PART TWO

Tuesday September 10 1974

There had never been a particular master plan but as he and Jean strolled to the back of her garden, taking in the late summer view over the cliffs and Channel and having a sneaky smoke before the family meal Mark accepted he really had no choice but to try – it was surely his destiny to at least do so. His fourth year lecturing at the university had been different in some quite significant ways. It wasn't as if he'd lost his enthusiasm for the students and even his subject, but the strain of keeping Justine happy while working on his relationship with Fiona's really very rich family had been taking its toll on him that summer. As he watched the slipstream of the Newhaven – Dieppe ferry, spreading out like two welcoming arms that widened as they merged into the deep colour of the Channel as it pulled out to the horizon, if anything he felt surprised how slowly it had come to him. It was maybe that he'd known somewhat subconsciously and all along when he had begun his pursuit of Fiona – after all, he had found out a little about her family before they'd even got together.

She had lived on the all-female floor above them during his third year at university; come to think of it, there'd been a few quite good looking girls up there. It had been a funny arrangement in their halls of residence – one floor for males and one for females, alternating up the whole block. Fiona and a good few of the others on her floor were studying some of the literature/arty courses on offer. As well as their paths having crossed quite a few times in the foyer and lift, Mark and his friends had spent many evenings hanging out in their communal living room after the bar had closed. His lot, the group he'd been thrown together with at the start of their course, had stuck together for the whole of their time at university and had persuaded the accommodation office to let them stay in the halls for their final year and to sort out a flat for all of them. They'd thought it would be a good strategy to be around campus when the new girls arrived and needed showing around. It had worked quite well, there had been quite a few nights trying to get some suitably obscure but definitely cool West Coast albums on between the Leonard Cohen and Carole King ones that virtually every girl on campus seemed to own, and that had become pretty difficult to avoid hearing drifting out of bedroom windows when passing any of the halls of residence, and particularly the female rooms in them. As it happened, along with Tom and the rest, Mark had spent various nights with most of the girls in the flat above them at different times. Fiona had been a bit more reserved than some of the others but he'd got her some dexxies one time and they'd spent the night starting and finishing assignments for their respective course. The Rolling Stones might have titled a song after the little yellow Dexedrine tablets when they recorded 'Mother's Little Helper' on one of their early albums, but they certainly helped students with getting essays done pretty efficiently. In fact come to think of it, his resultant effort on the strengths of symbolic interactionism had got him his only first class mark of the whole degree; and Fiona had raved on about her analysis of Scott Fitzgerald's role in twentieth-century American literature, which had also gone down well with her tutors.

What surprised him now was the memory that he'd spent an afternoon in the library pouring over a copy of *Debrett's* and some lists from *Forbes*, just to see whether any of the girls he'd come across at university were from well known, and thus apparently well off, families. In fact neither source had proved to be of any use – and anyway peers of the realm and their like probably had less access to ready resources than those who'd made their fortunes more recently, the supposedly nouveau riche. In the end, he had just asked Fiona, Paula, Annette and the rest of them where they had been to school; after all, sending your children to private schools was fast becoming a necessary sign of having 'arrived'. And it had struck him as more than likely that the newly rich would have less diverse and complicated family ties and so fewer family claims on any of their assets.

It turned out that Fiona had been to Roedean – looking back he wondered whether a jackpot line hadn't crossed his face. Indeed, that was why Gordon and Jean had retired to that part of Sussex and that side of Brighton, to keep alive memories of their daughter's school days and the attendant events they had visited there, as well as the walks on the under cliff path and the occasional celebratory meals in the Grand Hotel. It was odd that at the time he had no real idea why he had been researching the social background of his fellow female students. In retrospect it had all been done without any clear objective, rather a faint notion that it might prove useful. It reassured him in a funny sort of way to think, or, perhaps more probably, to pretend, that they were all fated to follow their destinies. Maybe he had been developing his own modus operandi even then. It was no wonder religion was such a wonderful excuse and panacea; and especially those forms of it which kept the mystical and magical elements to the fore and believed in all the rituals. It must be comforting to believe there really was a future and that it wasn't irrevocably linked to the past – much preferable to the varieties of puritanical Christianity, with their notions of success in one's earthly endeavours, in one's calling, determining futures beyond the grave and one's guarantee of salvation. The magical side of religion was much more interesting. It was a shame he couldn't rely on it for himself. He took the little comfort that his half-baked notion of predestination gave him; and after all and for what it was worth, his emerging plan, even if plan was perhaps putting it a little strongly, had the weight of many historical examples behind it. Inveigle your way into a well-established and extremely well-off family and consider the opportunities – no doubt a classic pattern, but maybe they were the best.

Of course there had always been the option that he could settle for a pretty comfortable and doubtless quite pleasant, and even rewarding, future but surely it was worth trying for a bit more – really that had been the problem, he'd always felt if there was more why shouldn't he get some of it?

His in-laws' family house certainly looked magnificent in the early autumnal evening colours. Mark was surprised Gordon had gone for a sprawling, Art Deco-inspired, quite modernist house; a Victorian or even Gothic pile would have seemed to suit his personality more. No doubt he had let Jean have a say in that decision, and it seemed to suit her fading and fast-becoming-tragic persona. Gordon had done well investing in the housing market after the war and his final move to this modern, well-appointed but still undoubtedly tasteful house, and really almost estate, on the outskirts of Rottingdean, had been well judged. It must be worth a fortune; but for all that neither of them seemed that contented, or at the least Jean's whole being was etched with boredom. It was as if because she'd got her way with the house and with furnishing it as she wished, she had lost the right to complain, or do anything other than exist there. Mark had always just about got along with Gordon, they'd avoided any real closeness, just keeping to civil chats about the Test Series and the merits of Ted Heath compared to Harold Wilson; and the lack of any close feeling, or maybe more accurately any real respect, was clearly mutual. Nonetheless, as long as Mark kept his daughter reasonably happy a grudging acceptance had developed. Gordon doted on his only daughter and while he'd always had his doubts about the worth of universities and certainly of the social sciences within them, he really had no idea about Mark's life or work. This left Mark considerable scope for subterfuge, a fact which certainly suited him. Gordon was obsessively and boringly keen to extol and emphasise the virtues of hard work and the enterprising spirit. He was proud to describe himself as a 'self-made' man, whatever that was, but it certainly made it impossible for him to enthuse about the promise of sociology. As far as Gordon was concerned, universities were privileged playgrounds that he'd been happy to indulge his daughter in but they were not places of any significance in his 'real' world.

Gordon was now well into his sixties and overweight; he'd worked hard and retired when he'd made more money than he knew how to spend. His tastes were modest but since he'd stopped travelling up and down to London, and had signed over and sold his estate agents offices in Knightsbridge, he'd decided to live as he'd imagined a Victorian patriarch might. To that end, after the heavy meal he insisted their part-time cook must provide at 6.30 each evening, he'd sit on the veranda, or at the full-length windows of the quaintly named drawing room, depending on the season. He liked the ritual, and even if Jean barely touched much of the food, he enjoyed it; and a large brandy or port along with, on occasion, his meerschaum or, more usually, a conventional briar pipe while taking in the view of the Channel gave him a contended glow. He kept in touch with the world and with his investments through the *Telegraph* and *Financial Times* and could reflect on a life with some purpose. In his more mellow moments the idea of Fiona taking over his estate and perhaps bringing up a family and his grandchildren here seemed quite appropriate. He was even prepared to consider that maybe universities weren't quite the waste of space that he'd always believed. At least Mark earned a reasonable salary and had a regular and, however unbelievable he might find it, an apparently relatively well-regarded and even high-status job as a university lecturer. Gordon knew that he would always be there to provide anything that Fiona might need, but he couldn't stand what he termed the idle rich, and it would have been anathema to him to support any kind of sponger or idle layabout, and he'd come across more than a few in his business dealings in the property market. All in all he had been quite happy to set Fiona and Mark up in the modest but quite substantial newish house just outside Black Rock and on the outskirts of the next village along, Ovingdean. Not too far away and a good place for any grandchildren that may come along. For Gordon it had been an investment, for Fiona and Mark a decent and cheap place for them to start married life.

Mark was well aware of how difficult it might have been to even contemplate the lifestyle that had brought him to this without Gordon's puritanical but essential generosity. It was perhaps ironic that the rent on Justine's flat and all the extras were basically courtesy of Gordon; a generosity which he'd been more than happy to accept. It had meant that he was left with a good salary and with next to no expenses beyond Justine. Having to marry rather than live with Fiona had been a small but worthwhile sacrifice, it was clearly the only way Gordon would have been prepared to fund their living arrangements. In retrospect, that afternoon in the university library had been quite well spent.

Mark looked back to the house and saw Gordon and Fiona sitting on the veranda under the arched doorway of the porch. It would have to be Jean first and then the old chap. The idea and then the details and possibilities had crept up on him. A few people he'd known had overdosed on drugs; if they could do so when they had some idea what they were doing, how much easier if the victim has no idea. It was the first time he'd thought in terms of a victim and it struck him that he'd have to justify it differently to himself at least. That wasn't too difficult philosophically or intellectually; time was a variable concept anyway and maybe a few weeks of revelry and pushing the limits might add more to Jean's path than a few years of the same monotonous existence she obviously felt her life had become. Anyway, how could one's experiences be ranked and measured against the dubious success accorded to greater longevity? It provided something of an acceptable and possible justification. Really, greater longevity wasn't any more a sensible measure of achievement than different and exciting and new experiences – quality of experience and length of existence were hardly comparable concepts. It was clear Jean was not the happy or even vivacious person she felt she should be and should have been; and he was pretty sure she'd enjoy some different experiences with him leading her on.

They'd stopped at the garden's boundary to look over the Channel and Mark turned his attention to Jean; he was relieved that she wasn't able to read his mind. How had it come to this? There had been two quite different parties – one at the end of the previous university year when he and Justine had begun their affair and the other a few weeks back at Tom's house-warming, when he'd realized, panicked really, that he might never be enough for her if things didn't change. They seemed now to Mark like signal events that had determined and laid out some sort of path he had to pursue; and he'd already started the preparations. There was no need to be reckless, but any more than a few months would be too difficult to manage without Justine, at the least, getting more than a little suspicious.

Surprisingly though, and a little irritatingly, he was actually developing quite a fondness for Jean. She was the sort of person who couldn't accept her ageing; and she and Gordon had grown apart – he was comfortable, large and happy to drift into indulgent obesity. Since Gordon's retirement they'd even taken to going on regular cruises of non-stop eating and drinking, although it had been drinking and smoking for her. She would do anything to stop the inevitable, to live again. Mark looked at her drawn face and cadaverous figure: she looked like she was wilting, the consequences of cigarettes and drink were engraved across and into her being. Their daughter, his wife, Fiona, had come along after years of trying and while Jean did love her daughter, neither childbirth nor motherhood had suited her. Of course, she had been provided with all the help she wanted in bringing up Fiona; Gordon had always treated her with generosity and care, indeed she could say that in material terms she'd had everything she wanted. But she lacked the social scene she had always craved, and now she had little more to look forward to than Fiona and Mark visiting; even the twice-yearly cruises Gordon sorted were becoming a chore. Hearing Mark tell her bits and pieces about the university lifestyle of the late 1960s and early 1970s and of the social scene in Brighton, along with the attention he paid her, sometimes seemed to make the years drop a little. She felt she had been living the life of a faded movie star without ever having had the thrill or excitement of being one. Past sixty and past her prime, her life hung somewhat abjectly on and around her.

Mark's strategy was developing almost without his directing it and so far it had been quite easy, locating and then preparing the natural poisons he'd found out about in a couple of visits to the library – under the pretext of looking for natural ways of getting stoned and how this might relate to his developing of a social deviance course. Although no one was likely to be interested in what he might be looking up in the library, to be convincing he knew he had to convince himself. He was used to this sort of distancing himself from his actions – after all, lecturing and by implication championing the thoughts and ideas of theorists you felt had added between nothing and little of merit to our understanding had had its effect. Especially when their words and quotes, heard from him for the first time, were dutifully cited and presented as significant and groundbreaking insights by year after year of easily impressed undergraduates. He doubted ethnomethodology or phenomenology would make a great deal of difference for the greater good of humanity.

So crushed castor beans became ricin and then part of Jean's shepherd's pie when she and Gordon had come over to their daughter and son-in-law's last week and he'd cooked his signature dish for them all. It had been straightforward enough, adding that into her plate when he did the serve up, plus a mixture of drugs that were pretty easy to come by on campus. There hadn't been any sort of immediate reaction and he hadn't expected one, but Mark had persuaded Fiona that they should visit her family more regularly now they were only a few miles away. He had offered to drive them over almost every other day over the last couple of weeks and before the new academic year had really got started. Each time, he'd made sure he had a mixture of something to add to the tea, whisky, gin, cake or whatever they were socialising over. And it seemed sensible to use small amounts and to mix the concoctions. As well as the ricin, of which he was quite proud – its almost antique status giving it, for him, a little more class – there were bits of psilocybin, barbiturates, heroin and really whatever was around. It wasn't a concern for some future post mortem, or any knowledge of properties and visibilities of different chemicals, it just seemed sensible to gradually, and from different fronts almost, weaken Jean until she would lose the strength to keep going.

It helped that Jean was hardly the most healthy sixty year old and that she seemed determined to make up for lost time; she'd been too old for the current drug scene and Gordon had stuck to all the rules when they were younger. From time to time they had socialized in London with some of Gordon's business acquaintances and contacts, but Gordon had never been one to flaunt his wealth and especially in the face of the post-war rationing and general austerity in Britain in the 1950s. They'd played at being upper class and dabbled in bridge evenings but Gordon had always run his estate agency business as a small but profitable enterprise and kept what he called the 'hangers-on' to a minimum. Jean had never resented his parsimony; she'd always been able to buy what she wanted. Nevertheless, there had still been an ever-present if almost submerged feeling that she should have had more fun; a feeling her son-in-law was managing to uncover and which she was liking.

As well as the additions to her diet and drinks, Mark had convinced her of the positive and enjoyable effects of getting high and encouraged her to have some pretty strong dope with him on the smoking breaks they regularly had together; and had also mixed up some cocaine and speed on the odd occasions they'd had a little time alone over the last few weeks. In fact it struck Mark that there might be something in the self-fulfilling prophecy idea that he'd struggled to find relevant examples of for the first year lectures on current social theory that he'd taken over after Dr Proctor's sudden retirement last Christmas. If he could convince Jean, and Gordon and Fiona, that she was looking unwell and needed if not medicine then some of the various, supposedly healthy, pick-me-up potions, there would be even more and better guises for a variety of less conventional drugs. And there were plenty of those potions around – Dr Pepper's and Metatone tonics were particularly prominent. It was as if everyone was feeling down, or else at least not up enough.

Mark was good at looking concerned and knew that Gordon, Fiona and Jean herself, for that matter, would be impressed by his caring for Jean when she would, surely, begin to react badly to things. It seemed too that being the first to show concern would in some way help the overall direction and strategy. The dilemma he pondered was that while it had to be a slow building up it had also to be sorted in terms of weeks and not drift into months. Then there would still be Gordon to deal with, at least. Really, he hadn't thought the whole thing through, but now that it had actually started he felt it would just have to unfold. It was maybe that once Fiona had control of all the family's assets, he would be able to ensure he had more than enough for him and Justine, and there'd be no need to concern himself over Fiona as well. The thought encouraged him: he and Fiona had maintained a sort of mutual understanding, if not respect. He didn't like to think of himself as some sort of crazed serial killer; as it was, he was just hastening his (and maybe even Fiona's too) access to what they would get sooner or later anyway. It was easier to rationalize now that Fiona seemed only to be going through the motions with him and rarely questioned his whereabouts.

He turned his attention to Jean.

'Wow Jean, you're looking great, really cool... I wish I'd met you twenty years ago.'

Jean loved it and loved him using these modern, hip phrases on her, after all she'd put on no weight and wasn't that the swinging sixties look?

She imagined the years slip away as Mark continued.

'Come and have a puff on this, we won't tell Gordon, or Fiona. You know, I wish she had your sense of fun.'

He'd added a bit of heroin to this one and made sure he didn't have much himself.

'Why not come down to Brighton with me sometime, it's too quiet for you here and I'll take you to a couple of hip places, with your style you'd fit in fine.'

She lapped it up.

'Would you Mark? I'd like that if you really think I'll be OK.'

'Of course you will be Jean, look I'm free Thursday and there's always a good night out in the Kings and Queens then.'

Jean felt odd but nice, the cliffs and sea seemed to be talking to her, and the clouds looked particularly enigmatic and understanding somehow. Why hadn't she been able to fulfil her potential and why not have some fun now? Gordon wouldn't begrudge her that and besides, there was no real need for him to know, he'd just assume it was a usual visit to their daughters, even though she knew that Fiona had been persuaded by Mark to spend more time with her various university friends. Mark had found out that Fiona's particular friend, Gill, had a new apartment and another one of her gang, Louise he thought, had become pregnant and he had encouraged her to keep in touch with them. Yes Thursday would be good, and it was only a couple of days away.

With the groundwork prepared Mark decided to arrange the night out with Jean. Meanwhile he returned to the present. The forecasters had got it right, thought Mark, the clouds rolling seawards over the South Downs from Lewes looked determined. This was it, a variety of methods and means, illnesses, drugs and poisons (maybe one day he'd write about it under that title, in fact it sounded like an album title come to think of it), without one causal factor and surely then there could be no direct trace or clear-cut case should it ever reach that stage.

Maybe too much reflection might not be sensible but he couldn't help analysing how it was all unfolding; really it was quite appalling how smoothly and quickly things had developed, but it was also pretty exhilarating. He was a little disturbed that he had taken over the persona of what he would have to describe as a natural born killer and all over one extended summer break when he'd avoided the usual round of conferences, summer schools and general toadying masquerading as networking that most of his colleagues were engaged with. What he liked was the way the ideas rolled in and the strategy developed, almost of its own accord. He'd written a couple of academic texts and prepared numerous talks and lectures, but this was a little like how he imagined writing a novel would be; with this next section or scene going to describe a natural storm, and his Morgan with the roof down and him prepared for it. Planned and executed to perfection. He could see why some of the serial killers he'd been reading about more recently – ostensibly as examples of dysfunctionality, lack of integration, anomie or whatever dull concept he was trying to explain and enliven to the year two theory students – kept records and cuttings of everything and developed a sort of storyboard approach to planning their next moves and crimes. It was clearly foolish and often the only means through which their convictions were ever secured, but Mark could understand the desire to produce a presentation, almost, around one's criminal activities; to explain to the world, or at least others, how clever and crazily rational the whole thing was.

He realized that he'd quite forgotten Jean, who was still gazing over the cliffs with a glazed expression highlighting the wrinkled upper lip. The deep lines from her nostrils testified to the effects of tobacco and nicotine, as did the slightly sunken eyes. He needed to get organized and get working.

'Come on Jean, let's go and have a little fun, nothing like a spin down the lanes round here when you're off your head.'

They headed back to the house and he propelled her toward the Morgan parked in the front drive with its top down in readiness. He'd used his first book advance and the promise of future royalty cheques to establish his image; and to keep up with the group of rich kids he'd spent three years at university in Canterbury with. Mark knew he could easily put up with a good soaking to see Jean shivering for the rest of the evening. Fiona and he had agreed to spend the evening with her and Gordon and help them entertain a couple of the neighbours; an old golf friend of Gordon's and his second, much younger, wife were coming in for drinks and nibbles. Jean wouldn't be able to resist trying to impress her neighbours and he knew she'd never dream of getting out of the ridiculous wiggle dress he'd spent the first ten minutes of today's visit raving about. Jean clearly bought expensive clothes but which somehow never seemed to completely fit or suit. Indeed, in Jean's case exposure of too much flesh had quite a disturbing effect, her décolletage evidenced the ravages of age and ill-health, her skin resembling an ageing walnut.

Mark was no expert in local weather but a decent chill could only help add to the strategy, and to the drugs and ricin for that matter. He'd have to up the amount next time and that scruffy third year on his culture course had promised he could get some barbital which was pretty lethal by all accounts. He knew he had to be patient and solicitous, it was all about impression management, but it was not going to be easy with Justine who wasn't going to hang around and miss out on any of her future plans for that long. He had to make some progress without Justine knowing and without those arses from last week's house-warming, and particularly Tom with his newly adopted country squire image, getting to her.

After he had inserted Jean into the passenger seat he put his head round the front door and shouted to Fiona.

'I'm going to take Jean for a spin up to Stanmer village, she's never been up there, what time are you doing tea for?'

Fiona was going to try out her new fondue on her parents and replied that it wouldn't be ready for an hour at least. Gordon was back indoors watching an afternoon play on the top of the range colour TV he'd finally succumbed to.

***

They pulled out of the driveway, through the oddly smiling and incongruous statues of lions that adorned the gateposts – how Gordon or Jean thought they matched the Art Deco style of the house he couldn't fathom – then onto the lane and up the hill towards the Downs and Falmer. It was his regular route to the University, up through Ovingdean with perhaps a slight detour through Rottingdean depending on how he felt, then onto the open Falmer Road, the B2123 through Woodingdean – an odd suburb that had expanded out from Brighton with a massive spate of council house building in the 1950s and '60s – but what a place to have a council house. It was strange how the Rottingdean area and more recently even Ovingdean had become quite posh if not gentrified. They had certainly lost the down-at-heel tag that had lumped them with the ill-named Peacehaven and the ramshackle collection of shacks, sheds and corrugated housing that had developed there a generation or two previously.

Mark decided to get a good way off straightaway so as to ensure a lengthy return journey. The car held the windy Sussex roads with ease, he passed the joint for Jean to light. In spite of her taut skin and her sallow colour, Jean looked to be in her element. As he got up to the A27 and Falmer he thought how much this part of Brighton meant to him too, he loved the town itself but also the outskirts and suburbs. Mark took a detour past the entrance to Moulscombe Wild Park where he'd taken Justine in the early days of their relationship and then out on the road to the University itself and Stanmer Park. Heading away from town, he turned left and swung in past the former lodge house that had been home to the gatekeeper of the Stanmer House estate before it was bought by Brighton Council in the late 1940s. There were a few cars pulled onto the winding drive up to the village but nothing like when the schools were off. He drove past a pretty down-at-heel looking pavilion, circuited the village green and church, and up to a row of what had been, and maybe still were, estate workers' cottages and the attendant gardener's sheds and garages. He turned the Morgan round and pulled in just beyond the church car park and suggested they take a stroll around. It was looking a fair bit greyer overhead but he may have to waste a few minutes at the least before the forecasted rain.

'It's so quaint, Jean; let's have a look around.'

Mark pushed open the heavy oak door of the picturesque, spired church just as he felt the first drops. Feigning an interest in the visitors' book, he spent a few minutes admiring the windows and ornate lectern before reminding her they'd agreed to be back within an hour. They walked back to the car and he opened the small passenger door, the rain was becoming a little steadier, pattering on the bonnet and small windscreen.

'That was lovely, Gordon was never really interested in anything other than property, prices and a bit of cricket and golf.'

Whatever the future might hold for her, Mark felt oddly pleased that Jean was enjoying herself and that he was the reason. He walked round to the back of the Morgan and fiddled with the catches on the soft top; now for a bit of play-acting. He wrenched half-heartedly at the supporting spokes.

'Damn, Jean, I can't seem to budge it today, that's the trouble with these collectors' cars. Look, we need to head back and you may get a drenching but it's better than waiting around here.'

There was no need to worry about her, he might as well have recited the Lords' Prayer, Jean looked enthralled by the whole adventure. These last few visits of Mark (and Fiona of course, but really it was Mark) had been the best few days she'd had all summer and beyond. She'd had quite a few stomach upsets and a feeling that she wasn't quite herself for most of the summer, and they seemed to be getting worse but she certainly didn't want to let them spoil things. The afternoons she'd spent with Mark, especially when Fiona had been away, or even when they'd just been chatting in her garden, had excited but also saddened her in almost equal measure. The conversations they'd had had been more personal and confessional than she was used to, and whatever Mark gave her helped her to loosen up in manner that took her back so many years. Somehow it all touched her memories and reignited the sensations of excitement and the dreams which had become lost in the everyday mundanity of life as, if she was honest about it, a bored housewife.

Jean remembered feeling herself as a free spirit in the early 1930s, before Gordon and the start of her comfortable future. It was now just her past and she recalled the nights she'd been persuaded by the two older girls from next door to her family's house in the less posh parts of West Hampstead to go into town with them and sneak into the jazz clubs just off Oxford Street. The feeling that she had missed out on important and no doubt illuminating things that had been happening all around her, while she was just treading water and adding years, was heightened by these recent experiences with Mark. Even the rain, now blowing into her face, appeared to have a different texture to it. Getting soaked in his car was almost certainly not the most sensible outcome, nonetheless the way her headscarf had blown in the wind as they'd pulled into the park and the admiring looks she had felt when they'd circuited the village made it most worthwhile. She wondered briefly whether this was what it might be like with a gigolo as escort. She wanted to reach over and feel Mark's thighs; well, he was her son-in-law. She left it just as a pleasant thought for the moment, enjoying a tingling in her own body that she hadn't felt for a good while now. Jean had done her duty sexually but had never really liked Gordon's body, or any man's really, they were such ungainly things, but here she was getting stoned and soaked and wondering about Mark's legs and, even though she could hardly bring herself to accept it, all the rest of his body too. If only she'd been growing up in the sixties; she was sure it would have suited her better.

* * *

It was a small sacrifice, thought Mark; the seats and floor would dry soon enough and there wouldn't be any permanent damage. He glanced across at her: the taut and stretched skin looked shiny and her dress clung desperately to her bony outline. By the time they pulled into the driveway again they were both soaked to their skins. Fiona had agreed that she and Mark would

73

stay for the evening to help out after her fondue; and as it could still be counted as summer holidays for Mark they were going to have a few drinks with the visitors later. And if they didn't feel like driving the few miles back to Ovingdean, they could stay over in the one of four spare guest rooms that anyway were rarely used by anyone except Fiona and Mark. It was these kinds of random opportunities, which he hadn't even engineered himself, which gave Mark a sort of fatalistic belief that his mission was inevitable. Maybe seeing it as a sign of some kind of calling would be stretching a point, but it was a little comforting too.

It had been a bit awkward to explain to Justine that he needed to spend some time with his in-laws given he had told her a good few times what he thought of them. In many ways it would be simpler to tell her everything and then they could work on it together. However, he wasn't convinced she would see it his way though – after all, she'd be able to find easier ways than the serial killing of her boyfriend's relations for getting the lifestyle she felt she deserved. He'd spent his supposed conference trip last week promising Justine that things would soon work out and that he was working on something that would change their life but that she must give him some time. He needed to follow up the drive with an evening and morning after here at Whitegates, working on Jean. He knew he had to start acting and doing rather than planning; but he also needed to spend some time with Justine when she came back from the latest family visit – which when he thought about it seemed to be occurring with greater regularity of late.

He drove the Morgan into one of the garages and helped Jean out.

'That dress looks even better after its outing in the rain, it's almost dry and you must keep it on, you'll soon dry out indoors.'

Mark had offered to prepare and pass the drinks around during and after dinner. He had brought enough ricin and barbital with him, which would pass unnoticed if Jean's glass were kept filled; and he could help with breakfast in the morning too. The crushed castor beans that produced the powdered form of ricin left a more distinct aftertaste and would be better used with the breakfast cereals and fry up which he thought he'd be able to persuade Jean to eat in spite of any diet plan or health kick she was currently following, but a few drops of barbital would mix well with any drinks and maybe a combination would disguise and mix up the effects anyway. He'd never pretended to have any great scientific or chemical knowledge but had done his research quite carefully and knew it would have to be a relatively slow process, and the best way would be to administer his concoctions as part of his role as a dutiful and caring son-in-law. One of the beauties of using castor beans to create ricin was that it could be utilized in a variety of different ways – in food but also rolled in cigarettes and joints. He knew Jean couldn't resist him offering her a little, individually rolled joint on one of their semi-secret smoking sessions. It was particularly useful that she definitely and desperately wanted to think she was walking on the wild side a little.

***

The evening itself had been pretty trying – in fact Mark was becoming somewhat disgusted with having to spend his time charming Jean. The guests from an even bigger and more ostentatious pile down the road were equally if not more boring. The second election of the year was on the horizon at the end of September and all the signs were that Harold Wilson would establish a proper majority and presumably a lengthy period in office. That had been enough to encourage a massive and massively ill-informed debate on the perils of socialism and the merits of Ted Heath. The odd mention of the oil crisis and three day week last winter had helped with the drinking and general expostulating and it has been easy to slip the barbital into the sherry Jean had started with, and later a couple of G and T's, although that was perhaps a little dodgy. Along with bourbon, gin and tonic was the one spirit Mark had enjoyed himself, but the clean taste wasn't quite so easy to tamper with. Nonetheless, Jean had had a few by the time he gave her the second dose. As well as the politics he had managed to have a good natter about the merits of Brian Clough and what had happened to make the his stay at Leeds so brief and apparently fraught; as with most people south of Watford Gap, they all hated Leeds anyway so it had been a little relief from the rest of the evening's conversation.

Mark had to keep reminding himself why he was doing this: he really needed a good night at least with Justine. This was becoming more of a strain than he'd envisaged and Justine wasn't too happy with his explanation as to why he couldn't go to a gig they'd been invited to at the Roundhouse in Camden. She had told Mark that was one of the reasons she'd upped and gone back home for few days, on the day of the gig in fact; of course , she did that trip a couple of times a year anyway so couldn't just blame him but he knew he couldn't risk giving her too much time on her own, she attracted too much attention. This had to be balanced, he knew that if he became too focused on the plan there was a danger that it might turn out to be all for nothing. For now he put that out of his mind – he'd sort things with Justine when she was back next week.

Meanwhile he had sorted a date, for the day after next, for Jean to come and have a bite to eat with him and a night out to listen to some jazz rock at the Basement Club, a favourite of his, on the Grand Parade just opposite Victoria Gardens. They had agreed that Jean might stay the night at Fiona and Mark's rather than get another taxi home and Gordon had been happy enough to indulge his wife – and probably to have a peaceful evening watching what he wanted to on the TV.

Fiona was quite pleased that Mark was making an effort with Jean , and she'd seen how worn and generally out of sorts her mum had looked recently – maybe a night with Mark and some music would be a nice tonic. Fortunately she had a long-standing arrangement to have a meal and a few drinks and one of the regular catch-ups with her University cronies. They were to meet at an apartment Gill and her boyfriend had just taken, overlooking the cricket ground in Hove, and with Gill's boyfriend away for a few days it'd be a nice girly evening. Really, and in spite of everything, Fiona thought it was nice of Mark to encourage her to spend time with her old friends and to be so understanding about her parents – and if he wanted to play around a bit it gave her more time to spend helping James at the shop. If she admitted it, Fiona was aware she was moving away from Mark, emotionally at least. Working with James had been good for her, she felt more like her own woman, whatever that meant.

Thursday September 12 1974

Mark looked out over the fields behind their house. He thought he could just make out the lights from the Beachy Head lighthouse, apparently still manned even though the new Regal Sovereign lighthouse, a few miles further out into the Channel, had been in action since 1971. He was expecting Jean any minute for their big night out – and one that would really test his resolve and acting. Fiona had gone for her girls' night out as planned, or maybe she was just using that as a cover for being with James; either way it suited Mark. He'd spent the afternoon preparing a shepherd's pie again –they could eat in before going into Brighton for the evening– simple but a really good cover for mixing in the concoction of castor and kidney beans he'd pulped down; and he could cook it in two little dishes which would look nice and be easy to manage, maybe with a touch of the thallium he'd found in a small chemists on one of his recent foraging missions. As part of his supposed research, he'd read about how thallium had been the poison of choice of Graham Young, who'd been convicted a few years back of poisoning something in the region of 70 people and had used it to hone his skills. Using different individual dishes reminded him of an Agatha Christie story, the detail of which he only vaguely remembered, but where the poisoned drink had been inadvertently switched and drunk by the wrong guest and so subsequently the wrong murder victim. He'd actually engineered it quite well at the drinks do at his in-laws the other night, although, come to think of it, it had been tempting to spike everyone else's drink as well as Jean's.

He saw Jean pull her little mini into the drive and totter out. What the hell was she wearing? It would have been acceptable at Woodstock maybe or more likely on Carnaby Street ten years ago. Her legs might have been shapely in previous decades but the bony knees and thick, varicose veins didn't suit a mini-skirted 60-plus year-old. Still, it wouldn't harm her to get more of a chill, or more to the point it would.

'Oh Mark I don't know what's wrong with me, I've never got any energy and just want to sleep when I'm home – maybe it's Gordon but I only feel any life when I'm with you and Fiona – and really especially you.'

That was a good start, and not surprising she wasn't feeling herself.

'Well we're going to have a great time Jean, you deserve it.' While you're still alive, Mark thought to himself.

He really was changing into heaven knows what, and wasn't too sure if he liked it. He knew it was all about objectivity and distancing, about goals and means. Really, it gave a little credibility and applicability to Robert Merton's notion of the innovatory deviant. Maybe Functionalist theory wasn't so off the mark, and certainly not as irrelevant as some of his departmental colleagues, or more correctly and if things went well his soon to be ex-colleagues, would have it.

He served the shepherd's pie and encouraged her to eat a decent amount, as preparation for a good night out he'd told her.

'Let's have a glass of wine and eat here first, and it'll give us some energy for later as well.'

Mark poured her a gin and tonic after they'd eaten, and made sure he had a couple of dexxies and a bit of veronal for later. He wasn't too happy at the thought of taking anything with Jean – maybe a half for him and the rest for her just so it wasn't too obvious. He probably needed to be someway stoned to cope with the evening anyway.

'I've ordered a cab for half seven but take this first Jean – it'll really help us get into the music and keep the drink under control.'

It was lucky that Jean was so easily persuadable.

'Mark I can't believe it, this is what I should have been doing years ago.'

Mark tried not to imagine Jean on a heavy dose of decent quality speed, it wouldn't be a good image. By the time they were dropped outside Victoria Gardens, at the entrance to the Basement, Jean was gabbing away at a disconcerting rate.

'I'm pretty good for my age, and I think I've a lot to offer still. I feel so alive.'

My God I hope the music is good, or else this is going to be pretty horrendous and pretty embarrassing, thought Mark.

The band had started their first set, more '60s British blues than jazz. As they struck up the first few distinctive chords from 'The House of the Rising Sun', Mark could see that Jean was already moving too quickly and getting some odd looks – or maybe it was the clothes that were. He ushered her out after a couple of songs and suggested a walk down on to the beach and a joint. To calm him down if not her.

They walked past the Royal Pavilion, crossed the Parade and then down the slipway just beyond the Palace Pier. Jean grabbed his arm and pulled him onto the beach. He managed to direct her back and onto a bench and lit up a joint, well it was pretty clear she would be up to take anything he offered her. The far too skimpy top exposed a deeply furrowed neck line and smaller lines below that petered down to her bra, this time reminding him of a railway map of Britain he'd had as a boy. The neck was so age defining, he thought. She had the look of a woman whose smoking and drinking had suddenly caught up with her and decided to expose themselves from the inside out. And too much sun had highlighted the ravages, searing them into her skin. The lights from the pier above added an unearthly, almost horrific touch.

'Do you think I look young for my age?'

Mark nodded and passed her the joint again.

'Let's get back and hear the second set then.'

He didn't mind her linking arms, and he reckoned he might even have to grin and bear it and let her kiss him. Still maybe time to slip the rest of the veronal into the next drink: that might calm things down. It was becoming quite a memory test trying to recall what was in each of the little packets he'd stuffed into various of his pockets.

The bar was pretty packed and there were some stoned people there. He hoped no-one recognized him: Jean looked like a sort of puppet cadaver as she swayed to the music. He propped her against a back wall and struggled to the bar. He ordered a couple more gin and tonics and slipped the barbiturate into Jean's. Time for one more push. He had to make the most of the night – he'd done a ricin-flavoured joint as well and wandered out with her across Victoria Gardens and to the back of the King and Queens. It was odd how little fuss was made about the obvious pot smoking that went on there. By the time they'd finished it, Jean was looking rather hideous and pretty wrecked; it was clearly time to get her back home.

He told her she was great fun and looked amazing for her age, and shimmied her round to the main road, luckily there was a taxi stand across the parade and only one other couple queuing. He really wasn't sure how much more of this he could do – it'd have to be ruthless and quick from now on. He needed to make sure Jean was ill enough for him to finish the first stage off. Mark let her slump against him in the back of the taxi and hoped she hadn't noticed the odd 'How's your mum?' looks the driver couldn't stop himself from giving him.

By the time he'd got her home and up to the guest room she was pretty well gone. He knew he had to make the most of the opportunity so persuaded her to have a nightcap and slipped the rest of the crushed ricin from his kitchen supply into a brandy and coke.

'That was great Jean, you're great company – and more fun than most of my colleagues, we'll do this more often if you'd like.'

Jean tried to put her arms round him as he slipped her under the blankets.

Lighting a final cigarette he opened the back door and looked down the hill onto the cliff top parade, he reckoned that was all he could have expected. Surely that must have hurried the process along. He couldn't take much more of it: he needed to sort Jean pretty quickly.

Friday September 13 1974

An auspicious date and day. Mark woke up early. Fiona had got in after him and was well away, breathing heavily, and Jean had slept in the spare bedroom. Jean must still be asleep so Mark put the kettle on and decided to wake her with a strong coffee – and maybe a little extra to help things along. He'd been sleeping badly and veering between a kind of euphoric satisfaction that came from the feeling he was controlling a whole series of lives and events, to an overpowering bleakness that it was all too much and why had he become embroiled in a mission like this.

He liked to believe he was a rational, reflective person and yet had never really analysed where he was going since Justine had taken over. He was just convinced he had to carry on, it was just his destiny maybe. Yes, he really was coming to believe it; and he knew he couldn't let doubts cloud his thinking. He put on their coffee machine and gazed out of the kitchen window as it hissed away. Even though the habit disgusted him he put a cigarette and lighter on the tray with Jean's coffee and pattered along the hall to the guest room.

Jean's cracked features broke into what he assumed was a smile rather than the grimace it more closely resembled.

'You're so good for me you know Mark... I know I'm not as young as I was but I do hope we can do this again.'

She looked awful. Mark put the tray down and sat on the bed. She pulled herself up: 'You know, I feel as if I'm not really here, my head seems fuzzy.'

Mark had told her not to worry and that he'd get her some aspirin or something stronger if he could.

Fortunately Jean's hypochondria was pretty well developed and if she started getting headaches, stomach pains and feeling drowsy he'd offer to see what the chemist might suggest, while looking appropriately concerned and wishing to help, of course.

'Look Jean, you do look off colour, let me pop into the village and ask the local chemist, he's always been really helpful when I've felt low. You stay here and later on you can have a little bit of the shepherd's pie I did last night, it'll perk you up. Fiona is around anyway and I won't be away too long.'

The fresh air hit him as he left the house, as if offering him a counterbalance to the miasma of his strategy. For the first time, Mark felt that this might actually happen and might not be too difficult. He drove along Marine Parade and up into the streets off the station. He didn't want to raise the suspicions of his local chemists and there were a couple of dubious practices in between Trafalgar Street and Gloucester Street that had become hippy hang-outs a few years ago; and where he'd been told by a couple of postgrads that a reasonable offer would get some pretty strong barbiturates with few questions asked, as long as he brought some legitimate creams and pills to boost up their official receipts.

It was a windy but bright early autumn morning. Mark needed a break before getting back to the task; he took a detour on his return and grabbed a parking spot on the top promenade. He crossed over and took the nearest slipway down to the lower parade, Madeira Drive. As he wandered past the shuttered ice cream and candy floss stalls, the deckchair stalls, still open but doing little business, and then onto the pebbled beach, he felt oddly comforted by the end-of-season air of desolation it all evoked. Picking up a flat pebble he skimmed it across the sea – too rough for more than a couple of bounces. He needed a little space to remind himself why this was actually happening – and it didn't take long: he knew he had to keep Justine and that would only happen if he offered her the best she could get. The collateral damage would be justified – and if some people might have to go before they got very old he was only stealing a smallish number of years, while dispensing some fun too.

***

Time to get back and press on. As he did so, Fiona had just arrived back from a quick shopping trip and was unpacking the bags as he wandered round the back. Mark realized he must have been away for longer than he thought.

'Oh my God, your mother looks poorly, I left her with something to eat and popped down the road for some advice from the chemist. Why not phone your dad and I'll see what I can get out of her?'

Jean was still in bed.

'Oh dear Jean, is it just the stomach pains? You look very tired and under the weather. Look, why not have a couple of these pills the chemist recommended? And then maybe you'll perk up and be able to come out again soon. It was great fun last night – and you know seeing some life and some live music might be just the tonic.'

Mark knew he had to balance the desperation for a quick result with a need to avoid suspicion but he had to apply a little pressure now. And it was a good time for Mark – it was not necessary to go into the university on a regular basis for a week or two so he could hang around and nurse Jean. He could also get the doctor to come out to see her – and the obvious diagnosis would be that catching a chill, plus a general weakness, was leading to a sort of natural deterioration. Then he could get whatever prescription was recommended and that'd be easy enough to mix with veronal or ricin.

'Look Fiona, I know your mum is well off colour but let's face it, she is a hypochondriac. If you're busy with the project for your work at the shop, I'll take her back home and she can leave her car here for now, you could drive it up to your folks when you're back. And I'll call Dr Evans and ask him to call in while doing his afternoon appointments, he's a sort of family friend anyway.'

Fiona wasn't difficult to persuade – really she'd never been that close to her mother and anyway she couldn't stand illnesses or ill people.

'Yes, good idea – maybe take her for drive along the cliff top on the way and try and perk her up a little.'

My God, even Fiona is helping with things, albeit unwittingly; and anyway, come to think of it, her project is refitting and decorating James's shop in the Lanes so he was hardly surprised. A wave of panic swept over him just momentarily; maybe that was inevitable.

'Give me half an hour and I'll run her home.'

Mark grabbed a quick coffee and went to get the Morgan ready. He managed to manoeuvre a pretty weak Jean into the rather impractical bucket front seat and drove the long way round, passing St Dunstan's, along the cliff top road and up through Rottingdean to his in-laws' house – the pretentious name Whitegates, cut into each of the gateposts, still irritated him even after all his visits.

Jean wasn't looking great and Mark told Gordon the doctor was calling in and that after that he could keep an eye on her and try and get her to rest and if possible go to bed. Sure enough Dr Evans called in and, as Mark had predicted, suggested Jean was clearly suffering the after effects of a chill which had led to a heavy cold and been exacerbated by her generally unhealthy lifestyle. Somewhat ironically, he had even said she was in good hands with Mark and Gordon there. After the doctor had had a cup of tea with them and left, Mark told Gordon he'd come back over the next day or two and help look after Jean. He needed to get out and clear his head; he knew there'd be a few of these moments and he knew he had to deal with them.

Summers had always been pretty good and pretty easy. Drifting from postgraduate study to a lecturing post had led to long and pretty self-indulgent Julys to Septembers. Nowadays all he had to do was tidy up the odd paper and lecturing notes but little more; however organising and executing a series of murders-cum-natural deaths hadn't been part of the usual summer activities. The pressure was getting to him and he wasn't used to feeling pressured. It wasn't any great moral awakening or concern; that was manageable, and really the challenge of doing it well and clearing up any trails and loose ends was beginning to feel quite exhilarating. The problem was balancing it all and doing it properly – which meant carefully and at the times and places he had control of, while at the same time keeping Justine happy. Finding time to act as a cross between a gigolo and doting son-in-law with Jean had made it difficult for him to keep arrangements with Justine. He had had to be ready to grasp any opportunity to spend time alone with Jean which had meant leaving Justine on her own for longer than they'd been used to over the last year or so. If he could have explained to Justine the reason behind it all maybe it would have been easier, but Justine hadn't given the impression she would be very understanding and had already been out and about on a few occasions with some old friends and, as he found out later, and apparently by chance, with his old university crowd, Tom included. In fact Justine had been behaving a little differently recently, she didn't seem to like him just popping in to grab a few minutes around shopping trips or other domestic arrangements. Being blissfully unaware of the real reason behind his slightly cloak and dagger behaviour, when she saw him she wanted proper attention and time, which he guessed was fair enough, but right now he could do with some understanding and flexibility too. He decided to book a table for the day Justine was back from another of her increasing number of trips away - tomorrow, he thought; he would try and persuade Fiona to spend some time with her folks over the next few days. It might help establishing the credibility of it all if Fiona realized quite how much her mother was deteriorating.

Saturday September 14 1974

It was two weeks since the August Bank Holiday weekend. He wasn't sure why it had been moved from the first week of August a couple of years back, and there were still a good few weeks before the students were due back. Mark needed a good night out and to spend some quality time with Justine. He knew she'd probably only got back an hour or so ago but what the hell, he was funding her to a considerable extent anyway. He drove down to the cliff top road, past Black Rock and on to the top parade, past Royal Crescent, still retaining its elegance and reputation as the poshest address in town, and still home to Laurence Olivier, Joan Plowright, John Clements and other thespians. He drove toward the aquarium before turning up Wentworth Street and onto Edward Street, then left to Devonshire Place. He pulled in a few doors away from their; after all it effectively was *their* flat.

'Come on, I'm taking you for lunch and a drink.'

Although she didn't appear up for it to the same extent as him, she seemed quite pleased he'd turned up. He sat down and flicked through the albums while she went to get ready. Mark half-sensed that there was something slightly different, he wondered if anyone else had been there before she'd gone away. He knew he had a tendency to paranoia but he definitely felt someone else had been there; maybe it was the album arrangements or just the atmosphere. Then again, he knew he must hide any desperation. He'd always prided himself on at least demonstrating a degree of coolness and confidence.

They ended up getting a sandwich and sitting on the beach just across from the Volks railway, still running although with only a handful of customers now. She snuggled up to him and said she'd missed him. 'Let's get a bottle and go back up.' It seemed as good as ever but Mark knew he had to get back to his plan and get on with things.

'Look Justine you're going to have to give me a little time, I have got a plan which will get us enough money to give all this up and sort things for us for good. I've always wanted more, you know that.'

He was surprised she didn't seem too interested in hearing any more. Maybe she'd heard it before or maybe she had her own plans. He needed her to understand.

'I can see you tonight. Fiona's going out so I'll be down later, let's go and have a few drinks in town.'

Everything he said was becoming just so hackneyed, like reading a self-help manual on how to plan an affair.

In fact he recalled later that the evening had in fact gone pretty well. There had been a few odd looks from the regulars at the King and Queens who'd seen him a couple of nights earlier with the bizarrely attired Jean; and there he was back with a pretty stunning replacement who must be two generations younger than the previous date. Mark had again tried to explain to Justine that he would have to spend some time away, and it would be worth it if his strategy was to work. Although she hadn't been too annoyed, she had pointed out that he had Fiona and wasn't the one always left on their own.

Well, there was no real choice: he needed to spend some time with Jean to speed up her inevitable decline, then he'd sort out any difficulties with Justine. After all, they still had quality sex together. He couldn't manage everything at the same time, it had to be one step at a time so something had to give.

Sunday September 15 1974

He'd stayed as late as he could at Justine's and got back in the early hours but Fiona hadn't appeared too bothered about that when they discussed her mother the following morning.

'I know you're worried about your mum and she really doesn't look good, but I'm around and got a pretty easy few days so you go off with for a break with Susan, Gill and the others if you want, you're going to have plenty of time to help your folks out later. It's easier for me before the term and teaching begins as well. And anyway, Dr Evans has been and checked on her too.'

Fiona looked pleased and surprised as well.

'What's got into you? You hate being up there and she is *my* mum, anyway.'

This was ideal, he could play the caring son-in-law:

'I know I go on about it but really it's not like that, it'll be nice to go and help your dad while Jean's so under the weather and spending so much time in bed. I can sit up there and read a couple of papers I've got to review, check out some draft dissertations from the postgrads. I do love the view from the patio, and it'll be a change.'

She didn't require any more persuading.

'OK, I'll go and pick Susan up but make sure you call me if anything happens. You've got Annette's number too if you need, but I'll phone you or dad's to check how things are.'

Mark didn't really care too much whether it was genuine or a cover. He'd use the couple of days to actually do something, he'd show Justine he was serious even if she wouldn't know he was pulling the strings; that description sounded better than becoming an apprentice serial killer. The gullible assistant to a controlling partner might have been tried by Myra Hindley and other gangsters' molls but he doubted Justine would see that as a particularly attractive quality, and certainly not one she hankered after.

He waved Fiona off, had a late morning joint and crushed up another few castor beans, grabbed the last few veronal and packed his work and a change of clothes into the Morgan. He'd have to cover his tracks better and make sure there were no traces or empty packets of the beans – he'd been pretty careful anyway, driving all over the area, even to Eastbourne and Hastings lately, buying them in small amounts. He needn't worry about the barbiturates as they'd been dealt illegally anyway and shouldn't be traceable. It was just one mistake that could blow it all – that was always the stumbling block to the perfect murder. There was no need for a mistake here though, the thing was that writing a crime thriller almost necessarily involved solving the crime – so there had to be at least one mistake. The heroes were the sleuths in fictional tales, they solved things, the Poirots, the Maigrets or the Holmeses. Maybe it was different in real life, maybe there were loads of perfect murders; and how could that ever be proved or disproved? It was no wonder crime and deviance had become the most popular and engaging area of sociology – even the statistics could be philosophised around. The most successful crimes could never be researched or written about because of their success, or rather they could be researched and written about but not with any guaranteed validity or a real understanding of how they managed to succeed. After all, the success was the mystery, the unknown quality. No doubt the statistics were fine for the crimes which had been solved, but then they were almost by definition the unsuccessful ones.

He arrived at Whitegates just before lunch and let himself in through the back door. Gordon seemed pleased to see him: 'Jean is not looking herself at all but I'm sure you'll cheer her up.'

'Yes, you take it easy Gordon, it's no problem, I've got some work with me and it's not busy at the university at the moment, and I've got some food from ours for both of you. As the doctor said, she just needs some time to throw things off.'

Mark had made sure he'd arrive in time for lunch. Charlotte, the part-time cook, was coming up to do the evening meal as she had done four or five times a week since Gordon and Jean had moved from London, and he wanted to act fast. He'd brought a couple of cans of cream of mushroom soup which he thought would be the best disguise.

'There you go Gordon, some soup and a roll; we'll have a drink after, maybe.' He might be puritanically inclined and dull, but Gordon had always kept a pretty impressive drinks cabinet, a sort of hangover from his days running the estate agency in London – the regular thank yous-cum-bribes were invariably bottles of good quality spirits and Gordon had kept to the habit of drinking the best since then. Mark hoped it might take the edge of his own nerves too.

'I'll take Jean's up to her after we've finished ours.' He carefully brushed all the crushed beans into her soup bowl and sprinkled a variety of bits and pieces from the herb rack over it.

Mark gulped his bowl down and took the tray up the sweeping staircase and onto the bedroom overlooking the grounds and beyond them, in the distance, the Channel. He pushed the door and stopped so abruptly the soup almost went. Jean looked an odd grey colour, not just faded glamour now but death warmed up, he thought. Maybe he'd actually done it already. It was a strange feeling. He sat on the edge of the bed, pulled the pillow up so Jean could sit upright and put the tray on her lap and told her how much he'd enjoyed their nights out and little ventures and how he knew they'd be out and about again soon. He couldn't help pondering whether the soup with all its additions would have dissolved the bedspread and sheets if she had spilt it by mistake.

'I'll read these papers and sit with you but you've got to promise to eat everything I've made you; it may not taste nice but it's what you need.' He almost managed to convince himself.

Mark spent most of the afternoon alternating between upstairs with Jean while trying to strike a balance by reassuring Gordon yet also hinting that Jean may not get through this and that if the worse should happen it was so good that he had his family and loved ones nearby; and that he'd be fine whatever transpired. He washed the dishes up and tided carefully and left at tea time before Charlotte arrived to do her usual desultory dust around and then cook the evening meal. Tomorrow had to be the day, the latest information he'd gleaned from ploughing through the whodunnits from Chandler, Simenon, Conan Doyle and the rest was that it didn't just have to be natural poisons or drugs: crushed glass in something sweet could kick start a final deterioration.

'I'll pop over tomorrow morning, Gordon: Fiona's away so I may even come up for a late breakfast. I love your garden this time of year, and anyway to be honest it's nice to have a little company.'

He didn't bother to articulate for Gordon's benefit the thought that marmalade and glass might be the best combination.

As he swung the Morgan down the drive, Mark experienced a surge of elation and power, mixed in with guilt for sure, but he felt pretty much in control and pretty good. He took a detour to go back through Rottingdean – he fancied a walk on the cliffs. He pulled in and parked in the little car park opposite the excellent fish and chip shop and café and the almost-ever-present ice cream van, still just about managing to do enough business to tick over even though the schools were back and the few tourists who did get as far as the village were down to a mere handful. Looking out over the Channel helped put it in perspective: what was one life, almost spent anyway, in all the vastness of this minuscule part of the country and planet? He thought about getting a drink on the way home, he needed someone to share the feeling of power with. Justine had said she was busy but what the hell, he'd go and wash and change and take a chance on it. He didn't want to spend the wait till tomorrow morning on his own anyway. It reminded him of the nervous anticipation he felt before an interview or even the first time he'd lectured to the whole of year one, the mixture of adrenalin and panic.

After a quick spruce up, he set off again. As he turned up from the seafront and grabbed the last parking spot on Devonshire Place, he couldn't believe it was less than a couple of months since the end of the academic year and his decision to make Justine his future, and getting quickly and seriously rich his new goal, and perfect murdering his new role. Difficult to believe it was only a year and a few weeks since that previous year's end of term party and his initial moves on her. That image worried him a little, it made him seem like some kind of besotted stalker. Putting the thought aside, he rang the bell.

Justine appeared looking a little flushed and rushed. 'I wasn't expecting you, I was just getting ready to go and see the girls from my final year.'

Mark apologised.

'I just needed to see you, it's been a hard few days with Fiona's folks and I've missed you.'

Justine followed Mark up, she wasn't too happy with the interruption but she knew how much Mark had helped her and he was looking quite vulnerable right now, she thought. She'd give him a little treat maybe and then get off on her regular catch up meeting with her friends, but better not mention that Tom had been on the phone when the bell had rung or that he had offered to buy them all a special tea at the elegant, late Victorian, Hotel Metropole later that afternoon. She'd realized straight away that her inclusion in the invitation was more than just an add-on; it was probably the reason for the event itself. Tom had hinted at the party that he'd like to take her and her uni friends out; and it obviously wasn't the friends he was interested in; presumably that was just to add a little respectability and no doubt make him feel less of a bastard, or maybe more appropriately with his background, less of a cad perhaps.

'Well I'm not out for an hour or so, how about opening a bottle and having a little quality time together?'

That was better, Mark thought he'd noticed a change in her mood but he accepted he was pretty poor at recognising moods or changes in them in anyone other than himself; and he wasn't too hot at that either. Justine put on his favourite Grateful Dead album, with 'Me and Bobby McGee' and the rest, and came back from the kitchen with the only bottle of wine she had, a Blue Nun left over from heaven knows when.

'Come on Mark, you spend more time with your in-laws than me. I need to have things to do as well.'

She pushed open the door into her bedroom and pulled him onto the double mattress on the floor. She'd always liked to sleep on the floor since having to spend the first term of her student days sharing a supposedly single room with Annette. She wanted this to be quick but nice and to send Mark away happy; and she knew she was pretty adept at doing that. He might not be all she wanted long-term but he had been good to her for sure.

Unbuttoning his trousers she squeezed him and knew he'd not be able to stay calm for much longer. Pulling open his trousers she bent her head down, kissing his chest and navel. 'Big Railroad Blues' merged into 'Playing in the Band'. She'd never needed or particularly wanted to overdo the oral sex, but today she decided to treat him. It didn't take long to get him ready and then she straddled over him, manoeuvred his cock into her and moved up and down rhythmically.

Mark realized this was why he was doing what he was. He laid back and let it all go. He normally prided himself on spending time looking after Justine's needs, but this was great.

'Bloody hell Justine that was nice, I couldn't help myself. I need to spend some more time with you.'

'I liked it too Mark, sometimes it's nice to just get shagged with no strings. You stay here for a bit while I get ready to go out.'

Mark wanted to spend the rest of the evening there but he could hardly argue after that session. Anyway, it would give him the chance to sort out what he had to do before tomorrow morning, before going to see to Jean – really for the last time if it was to work out according to plan. It all seemed a little more understandable and worthwhile as well, he thought; he couldn't throw this away.

He kissed Justine and told her to have a nice time with her mates:

'Look, I've got a few bits and pieces to do over the next day or so Justine, but you know I'm getting things sorted, things are going to be very different for you and me soon.'

He wanted to tell her and hoped the slightly elliptical and maybe mysterious hints and suggestions would heighten her interests. The fact of the matter was Justine didn't really seem to care too much; but then why should she if she had no idea what he was planning and how brilliantly he was getting there.

Mark drove off, feeling pretty damn good and pretty positive too: he'd do a bit of reading, a bit of preparation on the breakfast for Jean and have a quiet night.

Monday September 16 1974

It was another one of those bright clear early autumnal mornings. Mark pulled on to the cliff-top and then through a sleepy Rottingdean and up to Whitegates. Gordon was pottering around making his morning coffee in the kitchen. 'Jean isn't up yet, she doesn't look too good Mark, I popped my head round the door but she barely noticed.'

It was funny how at a certain age husbands and wives opted for separate rooms if they had the space. Mark tried to reassure him.

'Don't worry, I'll do her some toast and a cup of tea and take it up, you sit down and I'll let you know how she is.'

He mixed in the ground glass with some thick-cut marmalade and added the home-made ricin to her coffee. He couldn't fault Gordon's description. Sitting on the side of her bed he gave Jean a hug, feeling how weak she was. He told her he was taking over and she had to follow his advice. Firstly eat something and drink the coffee. She chewed with difficulty on the toast and he thought he saw a painful gulp as she swallowed. He reminded her of the good time they'd had together.

'You've had a good life you know Jean, and I've had a lot of fun with you these last few months.'

Yes this was it, she could hardly focus and wasn't taking anything in. He decided to take a different tack.

'Remember Jean, if you don't pull through you must reassure yourself that you've given us all lots of pleasures and I'd hate to think of you being anything other than what you have been to us, a beautiful woman, and especially to me recently, you know.'

He pushed on.

'You know I was pondering this the other day, I can never understand why anyone would choose to be buried, I'd prefer to remember people I loved just as they were, I'm certainly going to be cremated.'

He was laying it on a little, but Jean seemed to follow and nodded and murmured that she felt the same and if it came to it to let Gordon know.

'Oh that's just speculation Jean, you'll be out and about with me again in no time – anyway have a nap and we'll catch up later.'

Gordon was sitting in the living room, overlooking the garden and view over the Channel. It was amazing how he could immerse himself in the *Telegraph* while his wife was clearly dying. Mark gently took the paper from him, pulled up a chair and looked directly at him.

'It doesn't look good, maybe I'd better call Fiona in case she needs to get back here.'

He felt a brief wave of sympathy for Gordon.

'And look, if anything does happen you've got your family close by, and you'll know that Jean was happy down here with you these last few years.'

It was as if he was on autopilot, acting out a crime thriller which no one else was aware of; he needed to get out and have a smoke, even though he rarely did so in the day. He returned the *Telegraph* to Gordon and wandered down into the village and onto the under-cliff walk separating the pebbled beach from the chalk cliffs. The tide was out and there were only a few locals out with their dogs. He walked over the pebbles and onto the exposed rock pools. It was a long time since he'd played on a beach; he moved a few stones and watched the small crabs quickly bury themselves again. Pulling himself back to the task in hand, he knew he had to go back and see what was happening and give Fiona a call.

Gordon hadn't moved but was just staring out of the window, with the broadsheet pages of the *Telegraph* spread on the floor. Even he appeared aware that something was different this time. 'I haven't heard a sound from Jean, should we go and see how she is?'

Mark led the way. Jean was propped up on her pillow, although she looked the same she also looked calmer somehow. Mark knew she was dead. Gordon touched her face: 'What's the matter with her, Mark?'

'I'm sorry Gordon, Jean has left us.'

Mark had spent the rest of that afternoon with Gordon, and they'd been together while the doctor called and did his duties. Dr Evans knew the family well and was happy to fill out the details – natural causes, heart disease with a touch of emphysema. Fiona arrived back that evening and they took Gordon back to theirs. Fiona had moved into practical organizational mode which always helped. He called Justine and explained what had happened.

It was odd, he pondered. Justine had seemed somewhat distracted and when he'd said he would have to help out with the arrangements and may not be able to call round or even meet up at the university for a couple of days, she had been pretty understanding. He said he'd drop round as soon as he could get away.

In spite of his obvious shock, Gordon was full of praise for the way Mark had supported him and Jean. He agreed with him that they should respect Jean's wishes for a quick funeral and no burial. And Fiona was clearly pleased that Mark, for all his faults, appeared to be really trying to help her dad through things. In fact she was almost amazed at the conversation they'd had the night after her mum had died. Mark had pointed out that Gordon wouldn't be able to cope terribly well by himself and that they would have to be there to support him. He'd said that he was growing quite fond of the old chap and enjoyed the political arguments and banter so there was no problem him spending some more time up at the house with him. Maybe she'd misjudged him; and anyway it would give her time to spend helping James out at his shop. It was funny how one adopted euphemisms so as to feel better about things, she thought.

The funeral had been arranged quickly for the Friday after and had been a quiet affair. There was a service at the local church followed by cremation at the Downs Crematorium, just past Woodingdean and next to the Brighton Race Course. The family had on occasion attended services at St Margaret's, the quaint parish church of Rottingdean, dating back to the 11th century – indeed it was the church where Mark and Fiona had got married some years previously – and the vicar there had been most helpful in sorting the arrangements. Mark had been genuinely upset, an emotion he found strange to deal with given the circumstances. Gordon had taken it oddly: he acted appropriately and with some dignity but seemed unaware of what was actually happening. Mark couldn't help a fleeting thought that this might make it easier to carry on with his strategy – the only name he could accept for it all.

Monday September 23 1974

Mark hadn't seen Justine for over a week, but he needed a night out. He had plenty of brownie points with Fiona and it was time to look after himself.

Justine had missed him too; even if there were other distractions, it was a matter of pride – she wanted Mark to want her too. Perhaps surprisingly she was looking forward to him coming round later that afternoon – it had been pretty dull at university without him around. She certainly wasn't going to make things easy for Tom either, should anything happen in that direction.

Mark felt strangely energized and almost elated as he pulled up alongside the gardens between Devonshire Place and St James Avenue and parked the Morgan in the usual place.

He didn't yet think of himself as a killer, more that he'd controlled a situation and a destiny, and his own destiny too. However there'd be no point in leaving it at that. It had all gone so smoothly. He'd done some research into the likelihood of any investigation and sure enough autopsies for non-criminally suggested deaths were getting less common and had been for the last couple of decades; and especially if the family didn't press for one. Dr Evans had treated Jean for various ailments and concerns over the years and didn't approve of her drinking, smoking and what he saw as her general lack of self-care. Mark had impressed Gordon with his view that Jean would have hated to be cut open and examined and heart failure with perhaps a minor stroke had been the official result. Sure, a second death might not be so easy to pass off; but he'd think of something.

Justine looked pleased to see him. She pulled him to her on the doorstep in a way that only she seemed to manage. Mark felt he could talk at last, but he had to be careful.

'Really, they're just a drain on me and on society come to think of it. I've been back and forth for weeks and you know I wouldn't mind getting some of their money; and getting it before I leave Fiona. I really think we deserve it, Justine.'

Justine gave him an odd glance as she came back from the fridge with a bottle of wine. He sounded quite pleased with Jean's death. She put the thought away, maybe that was a little unfair. In fact she'd been quite taken with Mark's caring for his in-laws, after all he'd always gone on about how they were boring, snobbish old reactionaries with too much money and too little life. Justine had been surprised at the complete lack of any jealousy she harboured over Mark's family or the time he had to spend with them. If she was honest with herself she was starting to feel more and more relieved that it wasn't so intense between them. She liked being able to do her own thing – there was plenty to do in Brighton and Mark's friends, and especially Tom, were proving less hard work than Mark, and less obsessed with 'making it'. Maybe this summer and Mark's family problems had helped her realize she was becoming a bit stifled – she was 23, he was married and seemed to be becoming desperate. Justine knew herself pretty well and she knew that if she wasn't jealous of the time Mark spent away from her and them then that was some kind of indicator for her that maybe their relationship wasn't forever. She valued what she saw as her basic honesty and fairness. Sure, she knew Tom was keen on her, but also she hadn't really liked the sense of disloyalty she'd felt recently. She needed some time to see how things went and if Mark was actually serious about leaving Fiona. She poured a couple of glasses and started to roll a joint.

Still plenty of time to work through all that and she fancied an evening out and some nice food, and they were pretty good in bed too. Maybe she'd let him sort her out before they went out. She grabbed his hand and guided him through to the bedroom. He really was quite good at bringing her to a climax and seemed to enjoy it too. After she'd had finished, it didn't take long to manipulate him into her: she put her legs on his shoulders and pulled him in.

Mark didn't take long either: 'Wow I needed that, even if I could hardly contain myself.'

'Don't go on about it Mark, I just felt like feeling you inside me, let's go and eat.'

The rest of the evening had gone fine but had a slight dullness he wasn't used to, he couldn't put his finger on it but they seemed to have less to talk about. He was quite aware that it was probably because the main thing on his mind for most of the summer was off limits where Justine was concerned. He was bursting to tell her everything, to explain how brilliant he'd been, how everyone thought he was a caring, loving son-in-law and how no one knew him. Talking about anything else had started to seem pointless and irrelevant compared to the news he still couldn't reveal to her. He'd even mentioned how clever the splendidly named Dr John Bodkin Adams had been in his killing spree of the late 1950s and that it had happened in Eastbourne just along the coast, but Justine hadn't shown any interest. He'd also hinted that he was hoping to get enough money to set them up together, and very comfortably, but she'd just smiled and said money wasn't everything.

They'd finished off at the King and Queens and just crashed out back at the flat. It had been good but Mark knew he had to get on with the next stage; it was taking over, it was in his mind and dreams most of the time now. He knew Gordon would be a tough nut to crack, but maybe less so with Jean gone. He almost relished the challenge.

PART THREE

Saturday October 26 1974

It was a funny time of year: calendar-wise over three quarters of the way through it, but at the same time only a few weeks after the start of a new year for students and lecturers and academia in general, and before that of course for children and schools. For as long as Mark could remember his years had run from early autumn till summer. October was a transition time: the bright summer light had gone but the full colours of the autumn weren't fully established either. Today there'd been another heavy dew, which had cleared up by the late morning when Mark was ploughing his familiar route from Ovingdean, down the hill then up and through Rottingdean to keep Gordon company. It must have touched on freezing last night.

Since Jean's death, just over a month ago, things had settled down. The timetable at university had begun in its usual haphazard manner. His was pretty much the same as previous years but with some more postgrads to supervise. He'd met his new personal tutees, the quaintly-named freshers: a first individual meeting followed by the now obligatory university policy of an informal social evening, wine and cheese provided, which had been as excruciatingly embarrassing for all as ever. A couple of over-confident loudmouths, three or four quite pretty, young-looking girls who'd soon be taken with and by the usual predatory second and third year males, and a similar number of even younger-looking male students who'd have to wait a year or so before they could take on the worldly-wise stance with next year's newcomers. His first lectures had been reasonably well received but he had other plans on his mind and was really getting by on autopilot.

Justine was supposedly pursuing her doctoral research, but in a somewhat desultory manner, and with what seemed obvious to him less and less enthusiasm. Although it was not out of choice, Mark had seen more of her at the university than outside recently and had only been to the flat a couple of times since the beginning of term. She claimed to be busy and he was trying to focus on part two of the plan, Gordon. He'd spent more time with Gordon than Justine, come to think of it, and had been to see him almost every other day. He was going to suggest he'd stay over with him next week, when Fiona was off again with her mates, supposedly. There could be no holding back now: he knew he had to carry on and carry it through.

In fact, Gordon had been letting things go a little, which was probably a good sign. He'd taken to just slipping his dressing gown on at least for the morning, and not bothering to wear his previously ever-present tie, and not shaving so regularly either. Mark had been trying to hurry things along as well. There had to be a decent break after Jean of course, but that would have to be all if he didn't want everything he'd already done to turn out to be all for nothing. There was no reason, and he had no evidence, as to why he and Justine wouldn't make it; what he was finding difficult was not being able to share in the success of the first part of the master plan with her, or in the planning of the next stage either.

Anyway, he'd had enough of the almost constant self-examination: it had to be done. He pulled into the driveway of

Whitegates, the ridiculously grinning lions looking as out of place as ever. Letting himself in through the back door he breezed into the living room and greeted his father-in-law.

'Phew, getting nippy out there, how about a strong coffee Gordon?'

He used the filter machine Fiona and him had given Jean and Gordon last Christmas and added in the last of the thallium he had. He needed to get out and about to some different chemists. He brought a tray through and suggested they pull the chairs to the window.

'My goodness Gordon, the IRA are really putting it about; you know, Wilson's got to get a grip of things even if he has only got a few seats majority.'

Gordon was always happy to have a go at the Labour government, and really at politicians in general.

'Yes, bring back hanging for the bastards, but probably even Heath would never have got round to that; you know they're getting away with these bombing in the centre of London in broad daylight, it's a bloody disgrace.'

Gordon's support for Ted Heath had been wavering all year and even he was thinking it was perhaps time for the Tories to get a new leader.

'Anyway, never mind all that, how are you feeling Gordon and what would you like to do over the next few months?'

Gordon took a sip of his coffee. 'The thing is I'm getting on and haven't felt too good recently either, it's comforting to have you and Fiona around.'

It was strange but in a way Mark felt he was beginning to develop a fondness for the old chap, even if it wouldn't last for long; and Gordon had certainly warmed to Mark.

'You know I really appreciated how you helped Jean through her last few weeks, Mark, I think I may have misjudged you a little but you've got to indulge me for that. Fiona was our only child and she means everything to me, it's difficult seeing your little girl being looked after by anyone else.'

This was more like it, Gordon getting a little maudlin.

'Well I know Gordon, it's difficult because we have had different experiences and upbringings, and university life is not an easy fit with the financial and business environments you've been so successful in throughout your working life.'

Gordon weas clearly in reflective mode.

'The fact of the matter, Mark, is that when I sold the business and moved down here all I wanted was to spend the rest of my life with Jean, Fiona and latterly you of course. I was really quite relieved to miss having to wine and dine clients and keep up to speed with the ins and outs of the property market. To put it this way and looking back, you see Mark, I think Jean enjoyed it all more than I ever did. I don't mean the job as she never understood what was happening there anyway, just the lifestyle, the status, for what it was worth.'

Mark went across the room to the enormous, beech wood, bow-fronted sideboard that contained the array of spirits, liquors and mixers Gordon had always kept well stocked.

'How about a nip of bourbon to go with the coffee?' (He didn't bother to add 'and the thallium too'.)

'I think Jean was happier down here than you think Gordon, you shouldn't ever doubt that.'

Actually it wasn't really a lie, Mark thought – just she was happier down here living it up with me rather than vegetating in this pile. He poured them both a large Jack Daniels – it had been the one drink Mark had insisted Gordon had kept for his son-in-law and over the few years that he'd been part of the family he had persuaded Gordon to see it as a change from the scotch that had always been his favourite.

'Do you really think so, Mark? I felt she was becoming more distant and unhappy.'

Maybe time for a little flattery.

'Not at all. Of course, she liked to get into town more than you but she spent all her time reminiscing about the great life she'd had with you and how she owed you everything. You know, I think she just liked having someone to talk to about her life with you, which I'm sure is why she and I got on so well; and why we spent a little time together before she passed away.'

Gordon seemed pleased with the compliment.

'Never thought of it like that, I figured she was just bored, but that's interesting and nice of you to tell me.'

'You know, she'd have hated it to think of you just giving up. You owe it to her, and to your memories, to at the very least carry on living the good life and indulging yourself, it's what she would have wanted. After all, you've got the means to live well, so why not?'

It really was quite unbelievable how easy it was to persuade people to believe good things about themselves – but then he'd never had any difficulty, year by year, convincing each group of students they were the ones on the cutting edge of academia. Yes, the self-fulfilling prophecy was well worth applying to Gordon. Meanwhile Mark was increasingly aware that he had to work pretty smartly. Although he was regularly, and usually successfully, convincing himself that all was well, and especially so after each time they had sex, Justine was clearly getting irritated about, if not suspicious, of the amount of time he was spending with Fiona's family. Maybe she was noticing a change in his personality – after all, he was becoming wrapped up in the plan, but the difficulty was that it wasn't a shared one and Justine was nothing if not perceptive. Maybe that was what was actually happening and you just didn't notice your own personality changing. Mark had tried to avoid any over-analysis of his relationship with Justine but it kept creeping back to him: he knew he wanted her in a way and for a permanence he'd not felt before. It had started off as fun for sure, but had led to a kind of awakening and realization of how much you could get with and from someone. Justine had seen it as a fling and a bit daring to begin with and they'd both sort of pledged that that was it, but surely she was thinking the same as he did now. She had the flat and her research degree and a career ahead if she wanted; and he had helped all of that to happen too. Maybe this was his problem and he didn't want to face it, he thought he was special and deserved the best and couldn't imagine how Justine could feel any different. No, he reassured himself that she'd be fine, he had to believe that, and that he had to make it all happen.

Mark had always prided himself on never getting ill and always being ready for anything but the start of this last term had been more of a stress and struggle than he'd been used to and it wasn't down to the day job, it was more about what he was becoming. He was getting into the rather disturbing habit of waking in the middle of the night and going down to grab a drink to help him get off to sleep again. And creeping in and out of the bed he shared with his wife, he couldn't stop himself from wondering just how much better things would be with Justine and if it really would be that much different from Fiona. The more he knew he couldn't afford those sort of doubts the more they piled in to his semi sleeping thoughts. The reality was that there was no way back, he had blood on his hands already; but while that was all very well, it didn't stop the dreams or panics. Focus on the next stage, focus on what he had to do to get there, that was the only option.

It had been difficult to persuade Gordon to carry on eating well and drinking much, never mind excessively, since Jean's death and funeral, but the hours Mark had put in were beginning to pay off. He'd spent a few evenings drinking quite heavily with Gordon, while encouraging him to rant about the state of the Conservative party after the two election losses – and how anyone could vote for a devious pipe-smoking northern upstart like Wilson. Mark was not a great fan of the Labour party either but it seemed useful to watch Gordon getting redder and redder while they traded insults; and the prospect of him having to face up to it that Heath had had his day and that there was a real chance of a female leader of his beloved Tory party for the first time was adding insult to injury. In terms of his plan, Mark had even risked slipping a few bits of crushed castor beans and a couple of times a touch of veronal into the drinks. Come to think of it, he'd become a sort of waiter-cum-butler as well as debating partner. So within a couple of months Gordon was drinking more, eating less and ingesting gradually larger and larger amounts of the concoctions that had been used to lead to and cause his widower status.

In a way it had been easier when the term had started, as he was at the university at least a couple of days a week he could spend more afternoons with Justine and she'd agreed with him that he should spend more time with his family while Fiona and Gordon got over their loss. That was one of the things that attracted Mark, she always had the ability to empathise with situations and understand the feelings of others and wouldn't expect Mark to abandon them straight after such a trauma. Perhaps that was why it still seemed to Mark to be too risky to let Justine know that Gordon was next. He thought she might have been interested when he'd hinted that he and they would be extremely well off should it not be too long before Gordon followed his wife. He'd already indicated that the divorce he'd promised Justine would happen as soon as reasonable after Jean's death would leave him with a pretty decent settlement anyway. Justine wasn't stupid though and a settlement was just that – and even Mark was beginning to worry a little that Fiona might not prove quite as easy to manipulate as he'd assumed.

***

When he had been a student, Mark had never really studied crime or criminals in any sort of rigorous manner but he was warming to the notion of criminal careers and the arguments from the emerging 'new deviancy' theorists that some of his previous tutors and more recent colleagues were becoming pretty excited about. Interpretivism and interactionism were coming into their own in American and now British Sociology and he could see it relating to his own involvement in crime. It could easily apply to the serial murderer irrespective of whether or not it offered any absolute theoretical or philosophical explanation. The feeling of power and achievement in managing to have successfully disposed of a fellow human, while at the same time being almost congratulated over your part in it, was even quite rewarding. He could imagine the next one being easier to rationalise and easier to arrange too; and with both his wife's parents, in other words all her family, out of the way everything would go to Fiona, and the case for a better settlement for him would be that much the stronger.

In the early part of his career, Mark had never really reflected on where he was going but over the last few months he'd spent most of his intellectual energy and time doing just that. Last year's lectures and tutorials had been marginally updated to give an impression of engagement and interest; and it was easy enough to join the majority of his under-worked colleagues in the communal moaning about how hard they worked and how they spent every leisure hour thinking and reading and how no one understood the pressure of the academic life. Anyhow he was beginning to tire of that part of his life – it really was little more than a parody of the emperor's new clothes a lot of the time. Of course you had to keep your mind alert, but just a little bit of extra knowledge, a few points and ideas ahead of your students, an anecdote or two, all went a long way. In fact, there were few groups easier to manage or even con than undergraduates studying the great new endeavour of Sociology. The way the concept, as his colleagues would have called it, of labelling was seen as a key theoretical insight was almost risible. How could social life ever have existed without people forming impressions of those around them; and without those impressions having been influenced by time, place, current ideas and so on? And now academic careers and almost an industry were being built on some of the most obvious of concepts.

Apart from reflecting on his developing 'master status' – to acknowledge Becker's seminal work in the great new deviancy movement that was all the rage in Sociology at the time – Mark had become more expert in deriving poisons of varying degrees of potency. As well as castor beans, he'd been experimenting with and mixing in some of the pretty fantastic range of fairly lethal poisons readily available in various forms at various chemists. Also there was the bonus that through the monitoring of Jean's reaction he was pretty adept at assessing how effective they were in practice. As well as chemists, he'd travelled around the health shops of Brighton at first but more recently other towns around the South Coast and Kent, more out of a sense of being organised in his new role than anything else. It was pretty unlikely that shops or chemists for that matter noted whom they sold their kidney and castor beans, and more recently thallium, to anyway. Ricin was an entirely suitable product – he knew that even a small number of castor beans could produce enough to kill someone but only if it was inhaled or injected and although he was keen to get things sorted quickly, injecting his elderly father-in-law would not be either a feasible or a sensible strategy. Of course, the beauty of putting smallish amounts into the dinners that he'd offered to do for

Gordon now that Jean was gone was that the bouts of stomach cramp and the pains it lead to would come and go and could be controlled by Mark to some extent. He'd also learned that apple pips contained small amounts of cyanide, the classic poison of literature and history, and while it was unlikely Gordon would chew on a bowl of apple pips, if crushed up they could make a useful addition to the cocktail developing in Gordon's stomach. Although he had added the odd bit of coke or heroin it wasn't as easy to use more conventional, to him anyway, drugs with Gordon. He couldn't really suggest a night out smoking pot or flirt with him as he'd somehow managed to with Jean. On top of that, they were more traceable, which might be important as this was going to be the second death within a few months if all went well, so it had to be pretty well disguised; and as well as that and somewhat ironically, illegal drugs actually cost a lot more too.

As well as spending his supposed research time reading up on poisons, Mark had been particularly taken by a book he'd picked up on Graham Young, the so-called 'teacup poisoner', written by Young's sister and documenting his meticulous approach and relative success in killing or poisoning members of his family and work colleagues and managing to do this over a period of ten year in the 1960s and early '70s. Young had been able to collect an array of legitimate poisons from chemist shops in the south east of England, including in particular the metal-based substance, thallium, which had already made a useful addition to Mark's collection. Mark had convinced his colleagues at the university that his interest in murders and murderers would help him develop material for and help tutor the increasingly popular and understaffed crime and deviance options. He had suggested that they might be offered for both year 2 and 3 – and offering any extra options was a sound way to gain some credit and support from the rest of them. Really it was surprising how very few of the lecturers he had come across actually liked doing what their title suggested they were good at and paid for. Soon after he had started his lecturing job at Sussex he was struck by the way in which avoidance strategies were almost second nature, and there were always willing postgraduates happy to take on any teaching that could be off-loaded by the supposedly over-worked academics. Indeed, a little bit of funding for some kind of plausible research project could be used to pay someone else to take on a good few hours' tutoring.

Mark had also spent a bit of time reading up more on the reasons for and for not having autopsies after death. As luck would have it, and as he had found out after his mother-in-law's death, they were becoming less and less commonplace, partly due to the expense and partly because doctors felt they had the ability to determine causes of death – and didn't want to risk being proved wrong, no doubt. Mark reminded himself to drop that into the next chat with Gordon's family doctor, Dr Evans, who certainly was the type who'd feel he knew best and who had taken a shine to Mark for his diligent nursing and caring for Jean before her death (even if he didn't recognize it for what it was, murder).

Spicing up Gordon's food was easier when he visited his daughter and son-in-law and fortunately Gordon was delighted to have any excuse to leave his palatial spread and spend time with Fiona and Mark; he could ask his housekeeper to do his evening meal but eating it alone without Jean was a dispiriting experience. Mark's having found a sudden interest in gourmet cooking was an apparent stroke of luck for Gordon. Fiona was happy enough, Mark knew she would be pleased to have any excuse to spend longer in town, she'd even been taken to working almost full time hours as an assistant in James's shop, so was more than happy to have the cooking duties taken care of. Helping James out in the shop was an interesting euphemism, Mark pondered. Although Fiona had told him that keeping herself busy would help her get over the loss of her mother, he doubted that was the sole, or even main, motivation. Anyway so much the better, she'd be delighted to pay him off and it would even help ease his conscience a little; after all, if she found someone else she'd want a quick break and if her father had gone too she wouldn't have to face any disapproval over her not following the marriage vows.

Saturday November 23 1974

In many respects, Gordon had become much easier to manage than Jean. Mark didn't have to drive him around to pubs and clubs or spend hours pretending to enjoy his company. It was just a matter of persuading him to drink and eat as much as he could. And the amounts of each Gordon put away made it easier to dispense larger and larger amounts of ricin and the rest; while the brandies and whiskies were pretty good at disguising the veronal, amphetamine and other hippy/student drugs that happened to be around and come Mark's way. A large one after lunch had become the norm and Gordon's fast deteriorating taste buds hadn't seemed to notice the differences in flavour depending on the mixers available.

There was only a few more weeks teaching and then the Christmas break. That had to be it for Gordon; a heavy Christmas, lots of rich food and drink. Mark had to keep his strategy together. There were a couple of work do's – including the end of year departmental evening meal and drinks – and he had to spend some time with Justine, but the Christmas period itself, Gordon's first alone, would surely be the perfect opportunity for him to spend plenty of time with Mark and Fiona. He could suggest Justine spend some quality time with her family before he sorted things out with Fiona so that they could go public on their relationship, and if he could persuade Gordon to stay with him and his daughter in Ovingdean, he could do the breakfasts as well as plying the drinks. It was the ground glass that had helped finish Jean: that had to be the way, maybe around 28th or 29th of December, over eating and drinking and then a natural end. Mark could see it now, the understanding comments: 'It's funny how one often follows soon after the other, almost as if they wanted to be back together again.' He'd made sure that he had let Dr Evans know that Gordon was becoming more and more unhealthy, so had even managed to keep him sweet too, which was a bonus.

Wednesday December 18 1974

It was the first week of the Christmas vacation; and looking back, he should have been more aware of what were clearly pretty obvious signs. He'd hardly spoken to Sandra all term. The previous Friday, the last day of term before the Christmas break, had been odd. As usual the staff and postgrads had nibbles and drinks in the common room. He'd been collared by one of the research assistants who wanted some advice and help to set up interviews for her thesis on sexism in the academic workplace and after a couple of glasses had been quite distracted by her – Annette was tall and extremely thin, not his type if such a thing existed, but he found himself wondering what those long legs would feel like. He'd hardly noticed Sandra and Justine sitting together in the window seat and apart from the rest of them. While it was quite normal for lecturers and post-grads to mix, Justine hated Sandra for her snidey digs and what she termed her desperation and there was no love lost the other way around either. At the least the pair of them being together and apparently friendly should have made him think. After that the department staff had gone for a meal in town at the Old Ship Hotel. For some reason they'd done this for the last few years, a kind of recognition of it being supposedly the oldest hotel in Brighton. Justine could have come along as his guest even though she wasn't officially invited but had said she had things to get ready before Christmas anyway. They'd had a bit more than a cuddle in his office after the afternoon drinks and before he'd gone into town with the rest of them. He had been easily distracted as usual and hadn't got round to asking her what she and Sandra had been talking about. Justine joked about him chatting up Annette, before locking the door and pushing him into the old comfy chair he kept there to act out the role of the pensive, erudite academic when students came in to see him; she let him sort her out before sitting astride him and pulling him straight into her.

'There, that'll keep us going. Look, we'll go out after Christmas and then there's the big party at Tom's before we get back to work. I'm getting off now, I may get an earlier train home tomorrow so you have a good night.'

She could manipulate him at will: Mark had always thought he was pretty cool and pretty liberated, but Justine had real freedom and sensuality – she certainly put the stuff in *Playboy*, supposedly bespeaking of a new freedom and new man, and that he'd once thought cutting edge, in its place. He'd known that she loved the meetings and parties with his old uni friends; and he should have remembered that Stewart was putting on a Christmas party at his club which clashed with the department do. In fact Stewart had invited Mark and Justine some weeks back. Justine had said it would be fun but was fine when Mark thought they should go to their own department's end of term bash and, as she was going to see her family the next day for Christmas anyway, that really they would have to give it a miss. It had never crossed his mind that she probably avoided the departmental meal and went up to London on route to Carlisle and her family so as to catch the party at the club anyway and on the way. How come he hadn't learned anything about what really made her Justine after months of sleeping together? She would have put live music and a party at the Crawdaddy Club well ahead of sitting around discussing ethno-methodological issues and swapping departmental gossip.

Maybe the plan and implementing it and actually succeeding pretty well had taken over his whole being, or maybe she just sucked the sense out of him in more ways than one. He was in the throes of a double, at least, perfect murder plan, all for a future with her, but had somehow lost any real awareness of where Justine was in it all, or whether she would be there at all. He had just assumed that no-one could be as free and open with their body if they weren't as absolutely committed and convinced, and desperate no doubt, as he had been and still was.

Christmas 1974

Surprisingly but perhaps typically, none of those concerns had crossed his mind over the Christmas period that year: his focus had been all on the second murder. Gordon had spent Christmas and Boxing Day with him and Fiona; and somewhat disarmingly for Mark it had been quite pleasant. Fiona had pottered around doing some designs for the shop – apparently they'd got into selling posters and T-shirts as well as antiques and collectibles. James was clearly on the ball, and obviously after Fiona too, and the growing numbers of druggies and hippie types still flocking to Brighton would buy any old stuff as long as it had a few flowers and images of hairy men and/or ethereal females. Even though the commercialization of hippie culture might not be to everyone's taste and accusations of selling out were rife, it had clearly helped the market in attendant paraphernalia.

Mark had spent a lot of time drinking and eating with Gordon and watching whatever sport they could find on the television. In particular, they'd spent some enjoyable time listening to, watching highlights of and discussing the start of the 1974/75 Ashes series – Mark reckoned Lillee and Thomson would blow away Mike Denness and a fairly average England side; Gordon had taken strongly against this Australian team, uncouth, hairy and unsporting as he saw them.

Mark made sure he'd taken charge of a good deal of the cooking and all of the drink serving and had plied Gordon with mixtures of ricin, apple seed-cum-cyanide and even ground thallium in a variety of drinks and in that master of disguise, his speciality, shepherd's pie. It seemed to be having some effect, Gordon had a pretty constant stomach ache and cramps. Mark played the doctor and played it down telling him that at least he was enjoying yourself. He drove Gordon back the few miles to his home on the 28th; it was getting closer to the New Year and he knew he had to sort things out before his promise to see Justine on New Year's Eve. He told Gordon that he'd come round the next day and have lunch and tea with him.

'I don't mind and Fiona's busy with preparing for the January sales at the shop.'

He'd overheard Gordon saying to Fiona how much he appreciated what Mark was doing and how lucky she was to have him. It was certainly odd how he felt a growing closeness and even more empathy to Gordon than he ever had with Jean.

He was finding it harder to keep his distance emotionally, and was finding it hard to really understand what he was doing too. He'd always assumed that it would be more of a pleasure to get rid of Gordon; it was odd it just wasn't panning out that way.

Mark knew that the best strategy for him would be to cut out the now almost constant self-analysis – not least because the results were getting ever less flattering for him. Maybe he did deserve the best, why shouldn't he have what others seemed to have readily available? And so what if his comparatives were high, he had to hold on to the belief he deserved more: the basic premise that had led to this. He could appreciate the paradox, though. It had been strange: the more desperate to murder Gordon he'd become, the easier he had found it to be friendly and close to him and the better they had got on. Completely opposing directions which somehow married perfectly; the role of the caring murderer had really engaged him and it suited him as well as and in spite of the doubts. He had to finish it off on the 30th though, even if it meant putting Justine off for a day or two. They could go out later that week and had Tom's party on the horizon, even though he had a nagging feeling that there was a danger it could well turn out to be a double-edged pleasure.

The 30th of December had been difficult but ultimately quite satisfying. They'd had lunch and Mark had managed to use a couple of tabs of Valium he'd got hold of from one of the ageing hippies he was on nodding acquaintance with at the King and Queens. He'd mixed them up with remnants of ricin and thallium into the separate mince and onion pies he'd prepared at home the day before. Gordon was looking distinctly off before they ate and it was with some effort that Mark persuaded him that it was important to eat well. After eating they'd sat in the massive lounge: it still looked as chinzy as ever, the décor had obviously cost a fortune but had always succeeded in looking cheap. Mark had turned the heating up full and poured a couple of Jack Daniels. He kept Gordon awake as long as he could, he wanted to make sure and he wanted them to get through a couple more drinks at least.

'You know, I'm glad we've spent some time together this Christmas, Gordon, Jean would have appreciated it, you know she loved living up here.'

After all, there was no reason why Gordon shouldn't die happy. They chatted, or rather he kept Gordon marginally awake talking about MP John Stonehouse's sudden re-appearance in Australia and whether Lord Lucan was over there too. It amused Gordon that Stonehouse had been a Labour MP and hadn't even managed to disappear successfully. Mark knew he had to get on with it.

'Look, it seems to me like you need some rest. Come on, we'll go upstairs and I'll read the news to you.'

He guided Gordon upstairs and let him settle in the bed he'd helped Jean die in only a few months ago. Over the last few weeks Gordon had taken to using the bigger bedroom that previously had been Jean's preserve. Maybe it was so he could feel closer to his widow, but probably more likely because it was a nicer room and had a great view of the cliff tops and Channel beyond.

Mark needed to act quickly but also to get it all right. He phoned Fiona at the shop in town and told her Gordon didn't look good and had gone to bed; he said he'd stay and let her know if anything happened but not to worry, it was probably nothing.

He phoned the doctor's and managed to speak to Dr Evans in between his appointments. Mark explained how Gordon's eyes looked bloodshot but he was resting. Dr Evans advised him to try and give Gordon some aspirin and that he'd pop round after his late afternoon surgery. That had been a stroke of genius, Mark had been researching the effectiveness of autopsies and how easy it was to recognize and if necessary prove suffocation. If he could finish this off and persuade Evans there was no necessity for an autopsy it should be plain sailing. There had to be no bruising around the mouth or nose, and in Gordon's current state that should be avoidable; he was hardly likely to put up much of a fight. Bloodshot eyes were another symptom and that might be difficult to avoid of course, but then Gordon's eyes had been constantly bloodshot for as long as Mark could remember, after all he was halfway to being an alcoholic.

From then on it had all been according to plan. The actual smothering with a pillow had been easier than he thought, the poisons had been working for weeks and pretty virulently over the last few festive days. So poisoning and suffocation worked together and each mitigated the signs of the other to some extent. Mark was pleased he had worked on developing a good relationship with Dr Evans before, over and after Jean's death – he'd chatted about university life, the training doctors had to go through and the unhealthy lifestyle of the older generation, with Gordon held up as an excellent example.

Fortuitously, as it turned out he'd been right that Dr Evans had not wanted any interference or questioning of his professionalism and had considered an autopsy entirely unnecessary. They'd agreed that after a long life together one partner often followed soon after the other; and maybe that was the natural way of things. Even though Mark had managed to ensure that Fiona had just missed seeing her father before he died; when she had arrived and said her goodbye to his resting body, she'd agreed with the doctor and although obviously upset was also typically matter of fact about it all.

Wednesday January 8 1975

The funeral itself had passed without too much stress, although there was a new and nagging issue he may have to deal with. It had emerged at the after-funeral do which Fiona and he had put on.

Mark had used all his powers of persuasion to convince Fiona that her father would like the same send off as Jean, and would be happy for his ashes to be buried with hers. The funeral had been arranged and done within a week, on the afternoon of Monday the 6th. As it was their second within a few months Mark and Fiona knew the procedures pretty well, but it was still good going given the Bank Holidays over the new year. There had been a good gathering: some of Gordon's old staff and acquaintances had come up from London, as had his sister, Aunt Louise, who'd had little to do with him during his life; and him with her for that matter. Fiona was business-like as ever, she'd organised a spread at the old family home, and was busy planning how to get rid of the stuff her mum and dad had acquired and filled Whitegates with over the years. It wasn't that she didn't care, it was just the way of coping for her, no doubt. Mark and she had been getting on better over the Christmas period, and Fiona had been quite emotional and had seemed more vulnerable than he was used to when he'd called her and told her that her dad hadn't woken up on the penultimate day of the year. She said she couldn't have coped without Mark and the way he'd nursed both her mum and dad. Mark felt surprisingly moved, along with a touch of genuine sadness. It was odd – he'd done it, he'd effectively killed off two people within a few months and no-one appeared to suspect him; two people he hadn't actually disliked and had grown quite fond of. Now, after the event, it had all seemed so straightforward. There had only been one moment, just after

Boxing Day when Gordon took to his bed with stomach cramps, when Fiona had snapped at him and commented that his nursing and cooking abilities didn't seem to be doing that much good. Probably it was merely a throwaway line, but perhaps hiding a glimmer of suspicion, or maybe it had just been his paranoia.

The next step had been to help Fiona sort out Gordon's will: he knew he had to be patient there, and make sure he didn't look too eager. His main worry concerned Aunt Louise. As they were ushering the last of the mourners away after the funeral wake – come to think of it an odd phrase for the opposite of awakening – Gordon's sister had wandered across and made couple of comments that he could have done without.

'I gather you were a great support to Gordon and also Jean a few months back, but I must say it's funny how it all happened so quickly. I spoke to Gordon last year around Easter time after their latest Mediterranean cruise and he said they were both well and booking a world cruise for later in the year.'

Mark assumed that some flattery would be the best way of getting her off the subject.

'You never can tell, can you, but you must be a few years younger than your brother.'

Aunt Louise wasn't the kind of woman to be easily impressed.

'Kind of you to say so but I don't feel it. Anyway, I've offered to spend a few days down here and help Fiona with clearing the house and things.'

'Of course you must and that's good of you, let's shepherd the last of the hangers on away and then we can get on with things. I'm sure it will be a comfort to Fiona to have your support.'

He remembered that at the time he had a bad feeling about Aunt Louise: she wasn't going to be flannelled, that was for sure. However he needed to be realistic, after all she had only been a peripheral figure in her brother's life as far as Mark could tell.

Since Gordon's death he'd had a little difficulty trying to get away to spend any time with Justine and to see what she was up to. Although it was all part of the master plan, Gordon actually passing away on the day before New Year's Eve hadn't been the most convenient time. Mark had promised he'd spend New Year's Eve with Justine but hadn't become so obsessed that he felt he could leave Fiona to sort the undertakers and see to the moving of her dad's body, and then arranging the funeral itself. In fact, Fiona had said she had been planning to see friends on New Year's Eve herself, so she hadn't seemed over-happy with the timing either. He assumed that she hadn't been able to see the New Year in with James, masquerading no doubt as 'friends', just as he hadn't with Justine. He had always felt it odd how much significance was attached to who you happened to wake up with on the first of January of any particular year. Justine had seemed understanding enough but he sensed she was getting somewhat pissed off with, if not resigned to, coming second to his family. Of course, she didn't know it was all being done for her anyway. Even though he'd been hinting for weeks about the legacy cum settlement he'd have access to in the not too distant future, she'd seemed less than excited about it.

It was a lonely business and career path becoming a master criminal without having anyone to share it all with, or anyone to acknowledge just how well he was doing. Mark supposed it was in part because in his official career he was used to getting positive feedback, to adopt the academic vernacular; and here he was making a much more significant life change but without any of that confirmatory support.

Justine was certainly concerning him. He couldn't quite put his finger on it but even when they'd eventually met up for a night out on the 4th January, the Saturday a couple of days before the funeral, Justine hadn't had her usual verve or sparkle. Somewhat worryingly, she even seemed to be getting rather less materialistic and had mentioned travelling through Europe and Asia as a resolution she wanted to fulfil while she had the chance. They'd bickered more than usual that night: Justine had gone on about how much she was looking forward to Tom's upcoming party and didn't seem to appreciate that he had actually got away to see her while Gordon, his father-in-law after all, was waiting to be cremated. Maybe it was all too good to be actually happening.

Mark put this out of his mind. The whole motivation for the crazy path he was on had been because of his perceived need to shower Justine with everything the really well off, and that included some of his mates come to think of it, could have. They had made love, or perhaps to put it more accurately had sex, before they went out that night and again the next morning and it had been good – in a way it had just been technically good, in fact better and longer and more dexterous than ever perhaps, but lacking something nonetheless. Thinking back, it had been so well orchestrated it was almost like acting out a guide to extremely good sex, but it wasn't as messy and awkward and just not quite the same. More generally and if he was honest about it all, he was becoming increasingly obsessive and manic, and moody too; he wasn't able to relax in the way he had always prided himself on, he was hardly feeling laid-back.

Friday January 10 1975

Rather than build slowly on what had been a pretty spectacular few months, within a few days of Gordon's funeral, Mark found he had become consumed with the possibility of turning Fiona's losses and grief into her apparently natural death; though really her suicide would be more understandable. This was the last challenge surely – to engineer her suicide. Obviously another poisoning would be too risky; maybe Beachy Head, but he'd require an alibi. Of course, the fact that Beachy Head was a suicide hot spot, as well as being just down the road from them, would help. Accidents did happen, but this had to be 100 per cent believable and suicide would be easier to explain; it would have to look as if she'd just had enough and gone there of her own accord.

Looking back it had all been almost involuntary, one event – or, being honest about it, murder – forcing the next one on him. Good grief, perhaps being a murderer made you one – maybe this was defining and changing his personality and character. Although difficult to avoid, Mark was aware that any over-analysis or reflection would almost certainly be counter-productive. It might be unflattering to feel a loss of control, but the strategy was developing a momentum that wouldn't bear close scrutiny from him. He realized that sooner or later Justine would, for sure, pick up on it. Aside from their night out on 4th January, he hadn't spent much time with her, explaining he had to help sort out the estate and all his in-laws' things, plus the funeral arrangements. Still, there was a big party at Tom's coming up in a week or so.

Apart from keeping Justine happy, it had all gone spectacularly smoothly. There were still undercurrents of doubt though. He couldn't understand why he had got carried away with successfully engineering and completing the means to succeed with his plan without keeping his focus and eye on the ends, on Justine in this case. Even the will reading had gone off without hitch: in the end it was just Fiona, he and the family solicitor who'd met up on the day after Gordon's funeral – everything had gone to Fiona apart from a few specific items of furniture and pictures to Louise. No charitable foibles, it was all theirs – and if he could get anywhere near the half he was surely entitled to then it had been well worth it. He remembered that at the time that had seemed to be ideal – it was only in the following days that he realized that engineering a divorce and decent settlement would probably turn out to be a lot more hassle than a third and final death, which would leave him the appropriately desolated but rich remnant. He preferred to think of it as death rather than murder. The problem would be to play the grieving husband; and he'd need Justine's help and understanding to pull that off. There would clearly have to be a reasonable period of grieving before they could consider revealing their relationship to the world. He would certainly need her patience, and there were fewer and fewer signs of that; in fact, if he thought honestly about it he should have noticed that that particular quality appeared to be wearing thin with Justine.

Saturday January 18 1975

The reality was that any concerns over Justine's patience hadn't been foremost in his mind during the first two weeks of January 1975. Tom's party was at last a chance for Mark to get things sorted with Justine. He drove his usual route to Devonshire Place to pick her up for the trip over to the Downs and Ditchling. Mark needed to reassure himself that things were fine, or if he really had been missing the signs; he hadn't been out with Justine much for the last month or so but this party was maybe what they both needed. It was a sort of university reunion, plus engagement do at Tom's. Tom had been with Iona since he was seventeen and before his university days. He certainly hadn't been faithful then, in fact he and Tom had even shared a couple of girlfriends as some sort of post-hippy, free love recognition, and Mark was not convinced he'd changed that much since. He knew for sure that Tom certainly fancied Justine, even if he mightn't do anything about it in front of him.

He heard Justine come down the stairs and fiddle with the lock, reminding him that he still hadn't sorted the intercom. She had jeans and a close-fitting corset top on, pulled tight on her back and across her chest; she always knew how to outdo everyone – hippy stuff looked silly in early January, he reckoned this would set a trend. She had seemed to be in a good mood too.

It was a cold, frosty day with a heavy mist shrouding the countryside as they drove past Stanmer and the university and onto Ditchling Road, then up to the Downs themselves. They arrived early to give Mark a chance to catch up with Tom and a couple of other old university friends who were staying over too, and before the other guests arrived. Justine opened a bottle of wine and brought it over to join Mark, Tom, Pete and John around the large kitchen table as they reminisced.

'Come on Mark, aren't you fed up with university life – now you've married into money and acquired a stunning lover too?'

Pete had always been cheeky – maybe autistic in fact. Either way he clearly still had a great ability, or perhaps just lack of awareness, to put people under the spotlight.

'Let's face it, you only got into it 'cos of all the young girls hanging on your every word, you know you loved it.'

John joined in.

'Remember how jealous we were of the bloody lecturers, they had all the decent looking girls drooling over them, you know it's all about power, influence, money all rolled together.'

'Yes that flash politics guy, the one who took my tutor group, I found out that he'd been shagging bloody Judy with the great tits, the one I'd been after all of my first year, since week one just about. Good luck to him I say but at the time it made me sick.'

As ever with Tom, the party and evening was quite an event, the usual array and variety of drugs to keep everyone going with no expense spared. Justine looked great as always and as ever seemed to be at the centre of attention – Mark's increasing desperation to impress her and keep her had led him to some over-spending, both on her and on drugs, but also to some risk-taking. Not so much in any daredevil behaviour, but he was finding it almost impossible to keep his master plan to himself. He wanted her to know, he wanted some sort of admiration from her. He wanted to be congratulated for sure, but mostly he wanted her on his side.

Last time they had sex, he'd asked her if watching murders could turn people on; and he'd brought far more cocaine than usual from some local dealer who Steve in his year 3 group had introduced him to; and that more than anything had loosened the tongue.

He recalled that at the time she'd asked him why he was so interested in the disappearance of John Stonehouse and then the kidnapping of the heiress Lesley Whittle.

'Even the bloody Black Panther for heaven's sake, Mark; you're beginning to sound like a crime addict recently, you know.'

Mark had tried to rationalize it.

'Well the thing is I'm taking the new course in deviance and society and need the current illustrations – I need case studies to talk about. You know you've got to be able to apply the theory to case studies, to show how crime can provide status that can't be achieved elsewhere, how it can be a natural response to the situation.'

But even he hadn't really believed it so heaven knows how it had sounded to Justine.

The reunion party at Tom's hadn't ended that well, come to think of it. Both he and Justine had kind of built it up to be a big deal for them after Gordon's death and consequently the messed up Christmas and New Year plans. And the problem with greater expectations is that they usually led to greater disappointment. After a pretty heavy night, and into the next day, of partying, he'd had to persuade, or really force to be more accurate, Justine away from the rest of the partygoers before she was ready. They'd crashed out in one of the spare rooms just after dawn and the sex had been pretty perfunctory – Justine had just told him to get on with it, from what he could remember. Next morning or more accurately late lunchtime he'd noticed her and Tom chatting and smiling on the patio; he said his goodbyes and told Justine they needed to get away. Tom joked about them being lightweights and said they'd crashed out too early last night and Mark recalled him perhaps winking or maybe not at Justine as he opened the passenger door of the Morgan for her. He wondered now how many signs he might have missed, and how engrossed and oblivious to things he might have become.

Tuesday January 21 1975

A couple of days after Tom's party Mark had come back latish from helping box up and move some stuff from Gordon's and

Fiona had been asleep. He'd laid awake most of the night, sweating but desperate to finish the whole thing off. The following morning he'd got up early and driven to the cliffs near Peacehaven, he needed to get a grip and it was clear Fiona wasn't too bothered about him, so why should he care? She'd even encouraged him to go to Tom's and stay over last weekend. Fiona had gone back to work in James's shop soon after her dad's funeral and was spending more and more time there. So why shouldn't he finish the task? He felt could do almost anything: he had killed two wealthy but basically boring old people who happened to be his in-laws and also were the means to a future with his gorgeous mistress. He had executed a basically brilliant plan to set him and them up for life. He knew for sure that for his own sanity he needed to and so really had to tell Justine soon, and sooner rather than later. Mark needed her to be with him now. The problem with these moods of euphoric arrogance was that they never lasted long, and the periods of doubt and desperation were getting more regular.

What's wrong with me? They were nice enough; and Fiona too. Basically we were happy; and let's face it, the old crowd were frankly rather sickening when you really thought about them. What would his mum and dad think? He had a top job, according to the Register-General's scale, his future was assured and he had a wife with a rich and helpful family and really no obvious worries. Mark had thought of himself as a decent person too, but he knew he couldn't lose Justine, not now after this. The one thing he was sure of was he had to make it worthwhile – that would be the worst, for it all to add up to nothing. For all the planning, the subterfuge and now multiple deaths to prove pointless.

He'd driven along the coast road past Saltdean and on to Peacehaven and back, and admired the clifftop view, and the danger too, by the time Fiona came down and put some toast on and asked him to sit down.

'We have to sort out what to do about their house, Mark, and Aunt Louise is coming down sometime tomorrow to go through everything. I said she could have what she wanted, after all we've more than enough stuff.'

Really it had all gone pretty smoothly, but he could do without Louise casting aspersions. He'd met her for the first time at Gordon's funeral but she hadn't appeared as impressed as the rest of the mourners at the way he'd supported and befriended both Jean and Gordon during their illnesses. As well as that, she hadn't been easy to charm; he was normally pretty good with women of all ages, but Louise had been Head of a junior school somewhere near Croydon until her retirement a few years back and she was certainly no fool.

The only worry had been when the police had made what they called a routine call in the week after Gordon's death. They'd asked about his father-in-law's health and habits, and what he drank and ate but had gone away seemingly satisfied. Anyway, both Jean and now Gordon had been reduced to ashes. Mark knew that the tests scientists could do on exhumed bodies might be pretty amazing nowadays, but piles of dust would be beyond even them.

Wednesday January 22 1975

Louise and her husband, Oswald, had arranged to meet them at the house after lunch. It was a little over two weeks after Gordon's death and she and Fiona had agreed it was time and appropriate to do some clearing out. The most aptly named Oswald was a bony, ferrety-looking character: difficult to tell his age but he looked a good ten years older than Louise. Fiona had been talking about her and Mark moving up to the house, after getting it done up more to her taste of course, so she was quite happy for Aunt Louise and Oswald to rummage around and collect some furniture and knick-knacks to take away. Mark had offered to help them carry stuff to their car and they'd certainly taken advantage of things. Still, it was mostly stuff neither Fiona nor he would have wanted. There were oddly unsuited and assorted ornaments, some pictures that had been popular in the 1960s, but Gordon and Jean had certainly not embraced the 'retro-modern' style of that period. Mostly it was 1930s and '40s heavy porcelain pieces and dour paintings of landscapes; there were vases shaped like shells and jugs that doubled as china squirrels, dogs and other assorted creatures. They'd even taken what they could of the G-plan dining furniture and had earmarked the cabinet encased audio and record player, which may have been top of the range at the time but had clearly and rather depressingly had their day within a decade and looked distinctly out of place.

It was after Louise and Oswald had packed up, leaving the house looking like its secrets had been expunged for ever, that Mark realized he had to move ahead with the next stage but that he had to tell someone, and the only person he could was Justine. It had becoming too big a burden, it was consuming almost one hundred per cent of his energy and time.

He remembered it was something the strikingly cadaverous Oswald had said earlier in the day. He couldn't recall the exact words but essentially that they were a very wealthy and young couple, who probably had enough behind them to live a life of some luxury and little worry. It wasn't said in an obviously accusing way, but the implication was that they were almost too lucky – and it was all too good to be true. The tone more than his actual words that afternoon had just seemed to assume that

Fiona and Mark could never have really loved or cared for Gordon or Jean. Maybe it was because Oswald looked like he could never care for or empathize with anyone himself. Fiona had told him how Louise and Oswald had long ago stopped any kind of intimacy in their relationship and lived separate lives in separate beds. Oswald was certainly a funny character who had just sat there holding a china cup of tea and saying how murdering older relatives was the easiest way of getting rich and he was surprised more people didn't think of it. It was his disingenuity that made it sound simply a random observation and appear he was merely talking to a distant audience. Another of his comments about death and autopsies had stuck with Mark.

'You know there should be a mandatory autopsy for every death, I certainly want one for me; I can't understand why that doctor didn't bother with either of these two.'

Either he was autistic or a masterly exponent of allusion and insinuation.

After they'd gone Mark drove himself and Fiona back to their house in Ovingdean. They'd agreed to consider whether to move up to Rottingdean or just sell Whitegates and invest the money elsewhere. Maybe Fiona wanted rid of him; he'd never considered that either. He needed to see Justine and tell her what he was doing and had been doing and why it had to get sorted. He phoned her when Fiona was upstairs and arranged to see her tomorrow, there were still a good few days before the students were back and he told her he had something important to share with her. If she accepted it then it would all be fine, he didn't dwell on the other scenario that night. Maybe he should have been stronger, but he felt he was on the point of cracking; if Justine understood then it would work out. He had to know. It would be the defining and decisive moment but he couldn't put it off any longer.

Thursday January 23 1975

That was the day it all unravelled, and the reason he had been where he was for the last five and three-quarter years. Justine had done some lunch and they'd had a glass of wine and a smoke. Since the start of the year, she'd been pretty understanding about his in-laws and hadn't pressed him; even the odd comment about him not being around had come across as something she felt she should say, rather than something that she really felt. Nonetheless it was with some trepidation that Mark had pulled up in his usual spot on Devonshire Place that day. The apartment had seemed different, probably it hadn't been and no doubt it was just his anticipation of what was to come, but there had been something slightly strange about Justine's attitude and behaviour, a sort of detached interest. He hadn't wanted to confess all to her there, he recalled that he had wanted some fresh air and some space.

'Come on, we need to talk, let's go for a drive up to Stanmer Park. As I said, I've got something to tell you.'

Justine looked a bit put out but he'd been insistent and maybe she sensed this was important, or thinking back maybe she had thought he was going to tell her he'd sorted everything with Fiona and they could go public at last. Either way it certainly hadn't played out the way it should have done.

The conversation, it was perhaps more appropriate to call it the confession, happened by the church and overlooking the cricket pitch, a setting which evoked a string of memories from his childhood, as well as of the previous autumn, his drive there with Jean, and key role it had already played in his career as a poisoner. It had been brief. He'd rehearsed it through over the last few days and in painstaking detail in the early hours of that morning; but he never even managed to start it the way it had been planned.

Justine had surprised him by seeming almost over-concerned about how he had taken Gordon's death so soon after his mother-in-law. It threw him off the script. After all, she hadn't seem too bothered when they were at Tom's the previous weekend. He ploughed on anyway.

'You know everything I've done has been so we can be together and because I want the best for us. I don't want you having to work here or anywhere really and I don't want to spend another 30 years prattling on about social theory and methods. And I know you'd like and should have, and deserve as well, a good life with all you want, and there's no reason why we can't be like Tom and the others.'

He couldn't remember why he'd even mentioned Tom: that hadn't been part of his rehearsals. Justine clearly hadn't twigged though.

'I don't know why you're worrying about all of this Mark, I quite like things as they are and I know you've got to put your family first right now.'

This wasn't getting the message across to her at all.

'You do realize that I'd be pretty well off, really able to pack all this in for ever if Fiona and I split up and split up our inheritance. I've supported her and her family the last few years and she's got enough for both of us to be able to virtually retire on.'

'That's fine Mark but I don't want you to do that just for me.'

It was no good. The message, the confession, the pivotal moment he'd been worried about for weeks wasn't panning out at all as planned; obviously she had no idea what he had been up to. He had to push on, it had been time to tell.

'Look Justine, I've spent a good part of the last year planning to get my hands on Fiona's family money. Don't you realize Jean and Gordon didn't just die out of convenience? I've done it. I've spiked their food and drink with all sorts of stuff, I've become an expert on natural poisons and on illegal drug overdosing. I've engineered and carried out their deaths and no one suspects a thing. Don't you realize, I've planned and carried out the perfect series of crimes, of murders, and no one suspects a thing? I've done it all and for us and it's worked; and I've made sure that you've had absolutely no idea about any of it.'

It all came out in just the way he hadn't meant it to. There had been a stunned silence and she had just stared at him. He'd tried to get her to understand.

'I want you, and I want you to have everything you need, I've been away so much recently because I've been poisoning my in-laws. Didn't you have any idea? I've got away with murdering two people; and I'm going to do one more and then we'll be free to do what the hell we want. You must know, I'd do anything for you, you must have some idea.'

That was it then. Eventually Justine had spoken.

'Are you out of your mind? Anyway they were both ill for ages, you told me. They were old and unhealthy.'

'Yes and I made them. Look surely you guessed, why do you think I've been reading up on murders and poisoning?'

Mark knew then that he'd blown it. Justine lit a cigarette, which she never did in the day time, and never if it wasn't rolled into a joint. She had finally seemed to have taken it all in and was processing it.

'So that's why you were doing all that experimenting with beans and pips and the rest, and all the fascination with crime and murder. Oh my God, Mark, I can't believe it.'

She had looked at him as if he was crazy.

'And all that caring for them was just a big sham, oh my God, you must be mad.'

He'd tried to put his arm around her but she'd pulled away and stood looking out over the church graveyard and on to the park beyond and the great trees bereft of their foliage now. 'And what do you mean you're "going to do one more", one more who?'

Even though Justine was clearly shocked, Mark had gone on to explain that it would be natural for Fiona to be distraught and to do something that would be seen as out of character maybe but explainable certainly; and suicide could be pretty hard to distinguish from an accident and an accident, or any other means of death for that matter, wasn't difficult to arrange.

It was what happened next that threw him. She told him to take her straight back home as she needed time to think about it, but there was no way she was going to live with or hang out with him if he'd really done what he'd said; and a little incongruously given what he'd just told her, she said that anyway she was getting bored with their arrangement and relationship for what it was worth.

'Let's face it Mark, we may well have had a good time but I never encouraged you to do anything like this, I never signed up to a murder spree. What the hell do you think I'm like? It's never just the money for me, really you have no bloody idea. I'm not some kind of call girl; you've let me down. And if you are actually telling the truth you're despicable. I really can't believe it.'

He remembered clutching at straws even then.

'I've seen you having a good time with Tom, Stewart and the rest, I know you want the best and I was going to give it you and now I can.'

Something had happened to Justine since he had started on his confession,: her face and even colour had changed, the warm glow had frozen. It was a mixture of amazement and anger, and horror really. He wondered what he had actually expected from Justine, not necessarily a congratulatory kiss but surely some understanding if not admiration; and he wondered how he'd got it so spectacularly wrong.

'You really don't know me Mark, you've put me in an impossible position. Right now I wish I'd never met you, but this is for sure, you have to own up on this, you have to tell the police and Fiona; and you have to because I will if you don't.'

So it had not been the scenario or the response he had imagined. He recalled driving her back in near silence and leaving her outside the flat, maybe he had asked if he could come in but it was all a blur. He'd driven home and lit a cigarette, poured himself a large Jack Daniels and waited for Fiona to come back from the shop. He'd phoned Justine in some kind of desperate attempt to convince her and after the third or fourth time she'd answered. She seemed to have calmed down a little and said she couldn't be with him anymore but she would try and support and help if she could, but only if he took responsibility for things and told Fiona and the police. It crossed his mind that she had someone with her or had at least spoken to someone about it all. She told him that he'd put her in an absolutely impossible position and, again, that he must be crazy if he'd thought she wanted any of this.

Even though it had gone quite stunningly wrong, Mark clung to the hope that he might still be able to turn things around. His panic veered into anger, to hell with her, she'd had lots of good times with him and he'd basically supported her for the last year or so. He needed to try and convince her, and maybe she just needed to have time to put things into context a little. He poured himself another glass and, putting aside any doubt about her having company, decided to head back to Devonshire Place and Justine before Fiona re-appeared.

Pulling alongside the garden railings opposite number 32, the red Porsche parked in front of him looked familiar; he'd never really noticed other people's cars but knew Tom drove something similar. As he rang the bell, he noticed the curtains of Flat D move, but it wasn't that long since he'd dropped her back there anyway and why shouldn't she move her curtains. When Justine eventually appeared at the door, he pleaded with her to let him explain things. She said there was no way he was coming in to the flat but did agree to sit in the car with him. At the time, it hadn't really bothered him that it was probably because Tom was upstairs: his mind was racing, he needed to make her understand.

'You know I did it all for you, for us. We could have a great time together, we still could. I thought you and I were special.'

It was never going to work.

'We had some nice times sure, but I never signed up to you for life, I liked you but obviously not the way you imagined. And if you thought I'd want you to murder two people for me you must be bloody crazy. You can't put any of this on me, you're a double murderer and we're over. And by the way, we'd have been over soon anyway.'

She told him to get back and tell Fiona and then the police straightaway – and she'd be phoning his house later that evening to speak to Fiona and if he hadn't told her she would. Her final comment had stuck the knife in.

'You better not call me again, Mark, and anyway just to let you know I'm moving on and if things work out with someone else too.'

That had been it; he should have realized it but had been too obsessed to notice. He drove back in a daze. By the time Fiona appeared with some shopping he had had a couple more drinks; but even though part way drunk and still shocked, he knew it was all over for him. He just blurted it all out and told her to phone the police and ask for Sergeant White – and to let that bloody suspicious cow Louise and her feeble husband know that they'd been right all along.

Fiona's response had been rather different to Justine's. She couldn't believe it either but took a good deal more convincing that it had actually happened.

'I saw how close you were with them both, how much you cared. I was proud of you, maybe your mind is playing tricks, mum was ill and father wasn't the same once she'd gone. It was natural and it's natural for you to blame yourself.'

She really had had difficulty believing he'd done anything like it.

'I saw the doctor, I was there with them. It was natural causes, we all knew that.'

He'd had to tell her the actual details of how he'd done it, all of the planning, a blow by blow account.

'Look at these books on poisons, look at the amount of food and drinks I prepared for your dad, and do you really imagine I'd have wanted to go out and about in Brighton with your mum if it wasn't to get rid of her? It was embarrassing to say the least.'

Fiona had eventually taken it really badly. It was when she accepted it that her anger had really kicked in.

'I loved them, you bastard. I know you're a show-off and fake and I've never really trusted you, but this is something else: you're mad or evil or both.'

Somewhat incongruously she'd been holding a bottle of washing up liquid in her hand which she'd hurled at him.

'Come to think of it, you're so fucking big-headed you would think you'd get away with it. I've got to get away from you, whoever you really are.'

He remembered that she'd spat in his direction as she'd driven off, telling him she never wanted to see him again. He'd ended up having to call the police himself and wait for them to come and get him. Even they hadn't seemed to believe him at first and had been a little unwilling to take him into custody straight away.

***

The next couple of days had been spent at Brighton police station; he'd kept the details of it all to a minimum but provided enough evidence to tie the whole thing up. Even then he remembered how he thought it might be useful to keep some of the specifics to himself – for no particular reason he could think of, maybe for the court or maybe for the future.

And that was it. Remand, there was no chance of bail, a few visits from colleagues, more interested in gawping at him and the prison environment and pushing for an explanation he couldn't even think of himself. At least Mike, his head of department at the university, had offered to provide a character reference, but he sensed one or two others were almost basking in the kudos given from merely knowing a double murderer.

The divorce which Fiona had arranged and pushed through within a few months was a kind of blur. His solicitor had surprisingly been pretty helpful and sorted out a decent settlement (which he was awarded just after his sentencing four months later). In fact, Fiona hadn't made much of it and had just wanted it out of the way. Theoretically he could have argued for half of everything, although that was not going to happen and the deal that had been worked out had been quite reasonable given his situation. So half of the house he and Fiona jointly owned thanks to his father-in-law's generosity plus just under ten per cent of the rest would probably amount to a moderately decent sum of around £30,000. It had transpired that the family wealth was close on a quarter of a million; it seemed that no one, not even Jean or Fiona, had had any idea how much money Gordon had stashed away and how well he had invested it. Fiona had just wanted the house in Ovingdean sold and him paid off and out of the way and hadn't quibbled too much about the details. She was only twenty-five and a wealthy woman herself, and she and James were official by the time of Mark's trial; it seemed that she had just wanted to forget about him and move on.

The court case itself had excited national, as well as masses of local, media interest. He'd enjoyed the couple of days in court and had amused the galleries with his elegant, amusing, so he thought, and articulate description of the prolonged attempts to get rid of Jean and then Gordon. His guilty pleas had meant no jury to play to; and that meant he still had a lot more to embellish on should he ever want to. He was disappointed that the press hadn't come up with a title or name for him, presumably the varied, long-winded and often imprecise manner of his murders hadn't led to a natural title – he thought he'd keep the 'cocktail murderer' under his hat for the time being.

PART FOUR

October 1980 – Prison scenes

It was a chilly early October evening: the bell to signal the end of the first part of evening association had gone and the long termers and more elderly inmates were straggling back from the games room, the television room and sports hall to their rooms in the main block. Reflecting the fact that crime was a young man's pursuit, over 40 counted as old enough for the relative comfort of the main prison block; the younger ones who were doing short stints were filtering into the mixture of Second World War and newer purpose-built huts scattered around the other side of the prison site. Long termers meant anyone sentenced to three years or over, so included Mark. He had only been there since late February, but this early evening dispersal always evoked a pleasing picture, reminding him of something out of a Lowry painting. After the workshops had closed and tea had been dispensed the association period up to final roll call at 9 o'clock was characterized by a variety of movement and activity around the prison grounds. In the main it was just inmates circling the central lawn, typically in pairs or small groups planning their next, clearly dodgy activities. The new recruits looked bemused but generally still happy to be breathing some fresh air; the loners, the self-categorised semi-intellectuals and the dossers kept to themselves – the later swooping on any rollup ends that had been discarded before their owners had returned to their night quarters.

Mark was no doubt quite lucky to have been allocated to Ford Open Prison last winter, not quite five years into his life sentence; and in his favourite county and not far along the coast from Brighton. On the other hand his internment hadn't been unmanageable before then. The experience had made him reflect on how naturally and easily people adapted to their environments; mind you, even people taken hostage seemed to manage when they had to, there'd been a lot of talk of that since the holding of a group of American hostages in Iran the previous autumn. He had taken to the new, forced lifestyle quite easily, it hadn't been too bad after the first couple of weeks at the local prison, Lewes, and once he was allocated to the Isle of Wight. He had always had an easy manner and reasonable amount of charm and although the life sentence had been mandatory he had pleaded guilty, he had saved everyone, and especially the police, a lot of bother, and there hadn't been any violence in the conventional, gangster-style sense of the word. In fact, he'd got on pretty well with all but the most atavistic of prison staff and for that matter of inmates too. In terms of hierarchies and status amongst his criminal companions his crimes had earned him a degree of notoriety and even deference. Nonetheless, it had been a nice time to get out of the closed prison system, in time for late spring and the summer. Some of the inmates at Ford did seem to have a hard time dealing with the sense of freedom of an open prison, being able to see the outside world every day rather than on the odd working party, and being able, if they wanted, to walk out of it with a bit of planning and not too much aggravation. It seemed to offend their sense of being criminals and prisoners. Personally he couldn't see the point of trading a few months off the sentence for a future constantly looking over the shoulder, changing identities – a life on the run and all that would go with it. In most cases when someone went 'over the wall', which in reality seemed to involve walking up the road and not returning, it was to sort out some domestic issue, reacting to information about their loved ones, perhaps a 'Dear John' letter or some dubious issue that was felt to need their immediate attention. It had always amused Mark how it was deemed important, almost a matter of honour, that you had a reliable partner, a woman who'd be there for you, who was prepared to wait. However unrealistic, the pretence was an important part of many prisoners' identity; and it was highlighted in the desperation to be seen to have a presentable visitor every couple of weeks along with a regular supply of letters.

For him and most of the other long termers awaiting parole the open prison arrangements were a better way of ticking the time away and the fact it 'wasn't proper bird' was hardly an issue. Mark had got quite fond of the somewhat quaint, archaic prison argot that most of the regular as well as the small-time criminals down here and all over took on without seeming to acknowledge any sense of irony. In fact it had been difficult to have any sort of conversation with a good proportion of his current peers without a decent knowledge of the prison lingo. As far as Mark was concerned, being able to see a decent expanse of sky and a lot more green than he had for the last few years did make him appreciate things he'd never much thought about. It had been good to start playing cricket again and they'd had a couple of trips out to away fixtures that summer that he felt he could almost rank as among the most pleasant days of his life. There were no drugs or drink of course, but the looks and then conversations with players from local teams when they realized you could string a few sentences together had helped him feel almost normal again. Then there were the tea ladies who actually fitted the stereotype of English village cricket. It was nice to realize such people existed; and to see that, after a few minutes contact, they accepted our prison team as normal people rather than sex-starved convicts liable to put them in danger of imminent rape. Come to think of it, putting on a good few runs with Geoffrey, a recently arrived, and presumably corrupt, ex-dealer in prestige cars, at the annual game against the Duke of Norfolk's staff team in the grounds of Arundel castle was up there with anything he'd done previously. There had been the added nostalgia that he had been taken there by his parents when he must only have been about nine, to see the traditional game between the Duke of Norfolk's team and the touring cricket team of that year, in 1957 it had been the West Indies and he'd seen the famous Three W's in person and in action – Weekes, Walcott and Worrall.

Basically, it was all about adaptability; his conversations with a much wider spectrum of people had put the forced, intellectual, one-upmanship sparring of the university coffee breaks in the inappropriately named common room into the shade. Mark had enjoyed being a constant surprise to the various probation people, social workers, education officers and even those screws who weren't in it for a bit of bullying that he'd come across over the last five-plus years. When he had sat his first educational appraisal with a motley group of the recently convicted and sentenced at Lewes Prison, the first of his variety of venues, just filling the list of qualifications had led to the prison psychologist and the civilian education officer virtually falling over each other to call him into the office and suggest they'd find him a 'job' in the education wing or library as soon as they could. While that particular job had only been for a few weeks before his move to Wormwood Scrubs and then the Isle of Wight, it had set the tone for the majority of his prison experience.

Of course, since then there'd been some difficult moments. The first few months before he was allocated to Albany working prison on the Isle of Wight and after his initial stay at Lewes had been spent sharing time and sleeping arrangements with some fairly unsavoury characters in Wormwood Scrubs. Even then there'd been no real trouble; he'd shared a cell with a couple of pretty heavy-looking armed robbers for a few days but while he might not have been the typical con, a double murderer merited a decent amount of respect, as long as there was no sexual side to the crimes.

Albany had been interesting. It was re-establishing itself after almost a year's closure due to various riots and disturbances. The thing was that in spite of its reputation, Mark had never felt in any real danger while there. In fact what had always struck him most forcibly was the even stronger sense of deference and hierarchy among whichever oddly assorted group of humans he was incarcerated with than he had ever come across in his academic life. The notoriety and massive reporting of his crimes and the court proceedings, including, he'd like to think, his brief starring role in the witness box, had ensured a fair amount of respect from all but the most unhinged fellow time-servers he'd encountered. Even though he had pleaded guilty, he had managed to subvert his mitigation plea a little and had entertained the court with an outline of his strategy and some detail on how he'd managed to almost commit the perfect series of murders; and how he could have got away with it if he had wanted.

Mark had saved a lot of that detail from the police, who were happy enough with him admitting everything, but he'd made sure the court and mainly the press were offered at least a flavour of the full and florid detail. In retrospect it must always have been at the back of his mind that there might be some future benefit from not telling everything at the time. He remembered how the theatre of the court had impressed him, better fun than lecturing, and he had enjoyed a sort of last hurrah. Although he had lectured on crime and deviance, he'd never actually been to a crown court and the style and ritual, along with the eloquence, of the advocates had been a real and pleasant surprise.

There was one thing he'd never been able to answer or understand and that was why he had spent so much time and energy organizing what he thought was a pretty brilliant series of murders, keeping everything to himself and yet suddenly one day, after one disappointment, albeit major, he had changed his whole approach. Mind you, given that the whole purpose of it all had unravelled with Justine's reaction and response, maybe it was not so surprising. Really he had taken to the role of a public figure and master criminal with some relish. It had been quite illuminating, too, to realize that status could be unrelated to position or career or even maybe wealth, and that notoriety gave one greater long-term recognition and respect than almost any other conventional means. No wonder it was the outlaws rather than the law enforcers and apparatchiks who were the real heroes of gangster films and westerns. Generally speaking it was they who inspired the music of Dylan and the rest too.

It was just a shame they didn't televise court cases or even allow photos – and those court drawings were hardly glamorous. After all, since Mark had arrived at Ford Open Prison, he'd watched *Crown Court* on many of the afternoons while he'd been on hut cleaning duties and after his morning library stint. That series was great television, even if the real thing could be much better,

After his sentence, mandatory life of course, Mark had made sure to use his academic background and sociological training to help him deal with what he'd rationalised as merely the next section of his life. He never flaunted his notoriety, but let whoever his various contemporary inmate colleagues had happened to be find out bit by bit. It transpired that an ex-University lecturer wasn't that far removed from the peerage for the bulk of hapless offenders who'd also ended up sharing his custodial residences. Helping with petitions to the Home Office and letters to girlfriends and wives, along with assignments for the various vocational courses offered by the education wings, had provided him with a range of helpers-cum-protectors, should that ever prove necessary. As well as that he had made use of one of his early inspirational academic influences in adopting a mixture of the various possible adaptations to institutional life that Erving Goffman had categorized in his study of mental hospital patients a decade or so before this enforced time inside. Goffman had been one of the few social scientists whose writing Mark had found both readable and illuminating. In his terminology, Mark had tried to 'play it cool', to use the admittedly dreadful Americanization Goffman had adopted to characterize an approach of just doing enough to get by relatively unscathed. Really, the way in which Mark had coped with life in prison had all been a bit like the way he'd managed throughout his student days and, come to think of it, while lecturing at Sussex for those four years. Being the perfect inmate might have been a possible alternative strategy – to become 'colonized' as Goffman had put it, but that might have caused more hassle than keeping a low profile while not being overly awkward or confrontational. It never ceased to amaze him how much of life in general was prison-like in structure; it was just that the hierarchies and rules of everyday behaviour were given even more credence and followed more rigidly in prison than anywhere else he had encountered. It was fortunate that his crime and education had put him close to the top of the disparate and oddly composed pyramid that constituted the prison population.

Back in the main block, and as on most evenings since he'd been there, he made a final brew and settled down for the regular news night chat with Graham, John and Roger, and whoever else they let into their unofficial forum, before they would be shuffled off to their rooms soon after the 9 o'clock count. It was fair enough, the screws had to go home and rest too. Even though some of the middle-class, white-collar inmates resisted it, using some of the language had been unavoidable and had never bothered him – 'screws', 'the block', 'grass', 'ghosting', 'jam roll', 'bang up', 'red band' and so on were just part of the day-to-day language of that particular environment.

They'd all been at Ford for a while preparing for release after lengthy spells inside and one of the big outside issues they considered was what life under the new Thatcher regime would be like. It seemed to John that anything that was apparently so positive for private enterprise would also help anyone with a bit of imagination – and money of course. The reason those three were still there was partly because they had clearly not lost all they'd gained from their pre-prison activities. At the very least they could all have had a better chance of early parole if they'd been prepared to reveal and give up some of their different and certainly unregistered assets. Mark wasn't in that position, with no spectacular family money or criminal nest egg of his own – he'd been so close to it all but sorting the divorce settlement had not panned out quite the way he'd originally planned. The murder convictions put paid to any chance it would be based on his devotion and caring for his in-laws during their last days; and the needs of a life prisoner weren't deemed to merit a full share from his ex-wife's legacy and the family estate. Nevertheless, he hadn't done too badly from it all: Fiona was left with so much after the death (that always sounded better than murder) of both her parents that she was quite happy to pay him off. Her father had invested pretty well, so half the house he jointly owned thanks to Gordon's generosity had provided over five thousand pounds and just over ten per cent of the rest gave him a little over £30,000, a decent sum to invest for a few years. It had helped that he hadn't been able or even tempted to dip into it for the five years he'd been away; he'd kept an eye on the interest rates which had been good, between 7 and 10 per cent a year, and which had boosted it by a good 50 per cent overall.

Mark had got to know his particular group quite well – but in the typically guarded way they had all adopted, which never gave too much away. Even though they had formed quite a tight little network, they all knew they probably wouldn't bother with one another after their forced time together. Maybe that was what gave this clearly delineated period together a stronger sense of value. John, Graham and he had managed to arrange to spend their mornings in the education block following degree and postgraduate courses of one sort or another; and the evening meetings were a sort of follow on from that. Graham was financing himself to take a doctorate examining the theory and structure of white-collar crime and fiddles in the workplace – it would have been too close to home to study the manufacture and trade of LSD. His chemistry degree had served him well until the accidental discovery of his laboratory in an isolated Welsh farmhouse and he was adapting to, if not enjoying, reinventing himself as a social scientist. Eight years had been a long sentence; and did show that privilege had its limits. Graham's father was a pretty well-respected QC and his uncle a highly-regarded Permanent Secretary in the Home Office but that, perhaps surprisingly given the old boys' network, had only had a limited effect on the mitigation he'd received. John must be touching 60; he'd slowly opened up to them in their morning study sessions. It was ironic that one of the two former

155

Metropolitan police commanders it was said he'd been paying off for years was spending time at Ford too, but ex-Detective Chief Superintendent Kenneth Drury, previously in charge of the Flying Squad, was currently working for his privilege money in the industrial plant across the road, helping produce electrical circuit boards. He and other various police officers had generally had a harder time than Mark and the rest of the long termers over the years since Robert Mark's attempts to clean up the Met and the subsequent, well documented 'Fall of Scotland Yard'. You really were better off being a proper villain in prison. John never talked much of his outside life, but a number of disparate visitors appeared at regular intervals in a range of luxury cars that you could hear the screws talking about with a mixture of envy and disgust. He had owned and managed a number of dubious but clearly profitable clubs and bars in and around Wardour Street in Soho, which also attracted a mix of envy and disgust, although in the main a larger chunk of the former. John was due for release within a year even without parole and it was obvious he wouldn't be going short when he did leave.

Roger was the enigma – it had been in lots of ways the crime of the century; but they'd blown it by being too clever. The thing was, unlike Graham, John and even his own misdemeanours, Roger's had been hushed up – a D-notice had apparently been served and after the initial reports of tunnelling under shops in Baker Street and ransacking hundreds of safe boxes in a well-established and highly regarded merchant bank, the story had suddenly died. Rumours of compromising documents and photos, along with risks of undermining the government and embarrassing the royal family had circulated. Still, Roger had a good grasp of current politics and had just about served his sentence without even trying for parole, and he'd hinted he would soon have access to plenty of the proceeds. He was the archetypal cool operator but had been more talkative as his release date appeared on the horizon. That particular night's chat-cum-debate had been dominated by an escape the previous night by a couple of young drug dealers. John had started things off.

'So young Chris and his mate decided to clear off rather than wait for a knock-back. It seems a waste of two years and he'll be looking over his shoulder for ever.'

Escape was perhaps a rather exaggerated description. It would have been easy enough for any of them to have walked up the road and got well out of the way if they'd wanted. But it would have caused more problems in accessing their resources and keeping their family ties. Chris and Paul had been regular members of their debating group over the last couple of months since arriving at Ford in August and it miffed Graham in particular that he hadn't been told they'd spent their time there planning to avoid the wind-up of parole knock-backs. When they hadn't appeared for the evening association last night, no one had any idea they'd scrambled under the fence and no doubt been driven to one of the south coast ports and then the continent before the morning roll-call. Roger had been equally unimpressed.

'They may be too young for this sort of existence but they're still bloody stupid, they only got six years for close on a ton of the stuff. What did they expect? I'd call that a result.'

John had agreed.

'With their family support and good behaviour they'd have been out after two and half years, three max. Anyway we know why they spent so much time in the gym – getting ready for escaping no doubt, silly bastards.'

The evenings at Ford had an almost civilized feel and civilizing affect. Of course, though, it was still frustrating and nothing could capture the sense of dead time quite like the routine of prison life. Mark might have looked forward to the end of lectures and days and weeks and terms before but never in quite the same way as when the whole purpose, the whole context, was to count, tick off and so 'do' time. Mind you, he'd never worked in a factory beyond a few weeks' summer vacation job packing fruit after his first year at Kent, so perhaps he had no real comparable. However, it was manageable and even occasionally quite pleasant, and having a plan and an eye to the future helped. Mark had been pretty down for maybe the first year but that had passed, he assumed it must have been something about the proportion of time still to do in relation to what had been done and the difficulty of thinking about life beyond the sentence until you had come to grips with the whole time frame. He knew he'd been good at his university job and been good at his career move to poisoning and murder too. Really, if he'd had the proper support when it mattered, if Justine had had the sense to realize the benefits, it would have worked out fine; he wasn't going to make the same mistake again. Prison sharpened the obvious, you only live once and he wasn't going to let this stop him getting what he wanted and the life he believed, in fact knew, that he was owed. And he was only just 32, after all. On the face of it, he might have all the credentials of a one-off criminal and he was certainly seen as someone who ticked all the rehabilitation boxes, but Mark was determined to make up for the time wasted and with interest, and not to get caught out again.

In some ways he'd learned more from the last few months institutionalized in this part of Sussex and with these fellow travellers than from the closed-mindedness masquerading as academic liberalism he'd spent his first career engaging with. There it had all been highly respected and regarded for sure, but reminding him of just another version of the emperor's new clothes. Here the deviousness and self-serving was clearly and openly paraded. Everyone knew it was a game. This part of their lives had clear and absolute bookends, for those Mark thought of as his group anyway – the ones who had the nerve to take a risk and then the intelligence to succeed, to a certain extent anyway.

So maybe it hadn't been time wasted. Interspersed with backgammon and bridge tournaments there was a rough balance between prison gossip based around analyses of the characters and personalities of different screws, other staff and their fellow cons and a kind of television news or documentary style debate on current national and international news. They were all avid radio listeners and readers of the broadsheets and the analysis and discussion put to shame the departmental and management meetings Mark remembered from his university days.

The thing which no one who'd spent a fair time in prison could get to grips with was the changes that might have happened beyond the prison's walls, or fences in their case at on open prison down near the South Coast. It seemed to make the discussion and analysis more urgent and important, in spite of the reality that whatever happened on the outside there wasn't much that ever disturbed the vacuum of life as an inmate. It was strange that here they really were looking in on the world from outside. In reality, there was little that would affect their time inside, even if it might marginally reduce their assets and alter their outside contacts; they couldn't even vote but this seemed to sharpen the debate about political campaigns and positions. It was particularly since his move to Ford that Mark had recognized a kind of inverse correlation between being cut off from the outside world and being obsessed with discovering and discussing what was happening in it.

Mark hadn't taken so much notice when he was in the closed system; it had been a bit of a blur for the first couple of years.

A few things had caught his attention, mainly sporting events like Red Rum winning a third Grand National and then Queen Elizabeth's Silver Jubilee in 1977. But that kind of reflected the average prisoner's misplaced national pride and maybe racism, alongside an obsession with horse racing and gambling generally. Prisoners would gamble on anything and everything, with stakes of anything upward from half a roll-up. Of course there was also a fascination with any crime news. He recalled how the capture and trial of the 'Son of Sam', Berkowitz, had been passionately discussed. Then there'd been Elvis's death – and Keith Moon's which while not so widely mourned had upset Mark more. The thing he'd missed most was the 1978 World Cup – he'd watched the Dutch team before all this, come to think of it he and Gordon had watched a televised game when Holland were at their peak, with Cruyff and Johnny Rep and the rest pretty much unstoppable. He couldn't believe they'd lost to Argentina. That, as well as the rise of the new cricket phenomenon Ian Botham, had passed him by.

Since 1979, though, he'd become more and more passionate about knowing what was happening. Maybe it was Thatcher's election and the impact it had had which had been the spark; then there were the murders by and hunt for the Yorkshire Ripper, along with the almost risible police ineptitude in tracking him down. Anyway, he was certainly pretty clued up on local and world news, and the chance to mull things over with some fairly intelligent fellow residents over the last six months or so had been quite opportune.

Returning to that particular evening, the one after Chris and Paul had taken their leave and were probably having a drink or two in Amsterdam, he recalled how it had finished with a somewhat heated debate over the merits of capitalism, spelled out at the recent Tory conference in a speech the headlines had entitled 'The Lady's not for Turning'. There appeared to be a split among the Tories – some of whom obviously felt Thatcher's approach was helping deepen if not actually cause rising unemployment and continued recession; others who clearly didn't fancy any kind of disagreement with their fearsome leader. John of course loved her, he loved the way she had one hundred per cent belief in her own opinions. He loved her apparent lack of any kind of human touch or humility; and he loved her style too, she looked like a woman but acted like a man, 'a man's brain in a woman's body' was the phrase he'd come up with. Mark and Graham had thrown in the odd comment on delusions of grandeur, no empathy with any other views, paranoia of the self-made (wo)man and it had been a good bit of banter. Mark had seen another side to John too when he admitted fancying her and that he had even masturbated over her picture – prison had a crudifying effect on all of them, a sort of 'when in Rome' influence.

As the regular bridge and backgammon groups packed up their bits and pieces and before they dispersed to their rooms, Mark and Graham did a quick circuit of the main lawn, the regular wind-down they'd taken to over the last few weeks and which most of the prison officers were happy enough to allow them as they had proved no trouble in terms of prison management. Graham seemed particularly down. Mark had tried to cheer him up.

'It's really got to you those two buggering off, but you know Graham, you'll be alright – all this and the sentence you've done will give you a bit of infamy and star quality on the social circuits. You'll get the nod soon, I know.'

Graham wasn't convinced.

'Yes, but that could be next month but maybe not till next year the way it's going.'

'Look, you know it won't be long and what about me, I'll have to sell my story just to get started when I'm out. I'm sure you've got a decent amount stashed away.'

Graham said he'd help out and maybe they could do something together but Mark knew he'd have to plan for life after this by himself. He'd read enough and experienced enough about prison life. It was real enough when you were doing it but what happened inside didn't relate or translate to what happened after and outside. Although a lot of the small-time villains knew one another on the outside, there was no particular networking among the white-collar criminals. Anyway, he had almost enough from the divorce and the pretty reasonable interest rates to live comfortably for a while at least.

'Thanks for offering and maybe we will, but crime stories have always paid and I'll make sure mine does. There's always a market for notorious murderers: I can even see a film in it too.'

***

It seemed like a lifetime since he'd decided to tell Justine everything and then how she had forced him to own up and tell his story and face the consequences. In spite of that, it still gave him a sort of glow of satisfaction to think it was a crime or crimes that the police had never even been aware of and would never have been able to prove; and he was pretty sure that would never have changed if he had decided to keep quiet. The only detective work they'd actually done with any degree of success had involved verifying what he'd already told them. At the same time the years had merged into one and it seemed little time since his day in court. He regretted that his confession and guilty plea had meant he wasn't allowed the floor space that he felt he deserved to outline and explain his activities. Even though he had been given a little time in court while answering questions to amuse the gallery and press with an overview of it all, he had never got to spell out the detailed planning and thorough attention to avoiding forensic detection or proof he had managed. It irked him that he'd never been given the credit and acknowledgment for what had been close to criminal perfection. Although his fellow long termers rarely talked much about why they were there, Mark assumed they reflected on it all, as he had over his years inside. He'd held enough back from the police and trial to make a good story, he'd felt so at the time and was pretty sure that since then his mind hadn't become so self-obsessed or addled that he was wrong about there being some real potential in it. The initial publicity had given him a few days in the media spotlight and the people he'd talked to over the years since had certainly given the impression of being engrossed and impressed as well. After all, two murders put him in a pretty elite category in any criminal hierarchy.

He still wasn't sure why he'd confessed or why he'd recently decided he would write about it all and try to make something out of it. The confession had probably been inevitable. After he'd succeeded in executing the plan and as he saw Fiona taking charge of the family mansion and estate, the strain of having virtually changed just about his whole identity and of knowing he'd killed two people, while at the same time having been congratulated for the way he'd cared for them, was becoming too much. However the real reason he couldn't carry it off was down to his almost unbelievable misjudgement of how Justine would take it all. He had known all along that he'd have to tell Justine eventually and he knew at the time that he just had to talk it over with someone. The whole thing had just become too all-consuming and he was beginning to lose sight of the point of it, so really it had to be Justine he told. The thing was he had imagined how it would play out quite differently –

Justine should have been excited and even turned on by it all, she should have embraced being a party to it all. It should have set them up for a life together.

Looking back, if he was honest about it, he'd also been aware that there were a few questions being asked. Even if not enough to have put him in any real danger of being uncovered, the pressure on him was perhaps not solely of his own making. It maybe wasn't the classic 'hell have no fury like a woman scorned', but his one-time lover and colleague at Sussex University, Sandra, hadn't been over-happy with him devoting all his spare time to Justine and had hinted at her suspicions after Gordon had died. When a couple of Sussex's CID officers had politely asked if they could have an 'off the record' chat, he'd guessed Sandra had either passed on her suspicions to one of her contacts in the local police or, more likely, had done as much to Fiona's aunt who'd appeared with increasing regularity, initially, he re-called, after her sister-in-law's death and even more so after her brother, Gordon, had followed suit. Now, come to think of it, he vaguely remembered her and Sandra sitting on the veranda together after one of the funerals.

Mark had denied all knowledge at first and had started to help set up a plausibly false trail based on an account of his in-laws following a dysfunctional retirement life that included hypochondria, over-medicating, overdosing and over-indulging. In fact it seemed to be going down well with no sign of Her Majesty's finest doubting his devotion to his family, and it was certainly filling a few pages of their notebooks. However Mark lost interest in any excuses or really in getting away with it after Justine drifted away – or perhaps more accurately jumped ship with alacrity. After all, the intention had been to ride off into the future with her. Unusually, really, given all the care he'd put into planning and carrying it all through, when

Justine pretty much freaked out, he had his own 'what the hell' moment and he had wanted to make the most of it.

He certainly made the most of his story when he called DI Wilson and his sidekick, DC Wallace, back just a few days after their initial routine visit and note-taking and the morning after he'd confessed to Justine and later Fiona. It really did just fall apart that quickly, and that was one thing he had never been able to explain to himself over the years he'd been away, he didn't recognize it as part of his character or style. It must have been a brainstorm, a cry for help even though that didn't fit his understanding of himself and his own personality. He had conceived a brilliant plan and then made a spectacular success of carrying it out; he just hadn't been able to keep it himself.

In retrospect, and surprisingly, the police hadn't been all that willing to take him into custody at first. Thinking back on it, they really had not seemed to believe him, although eventually they had agreed that the best thing was to take him to the station for more detailed questioning. They had seemed so surprised if not dubious that they had even let him call in at the university on the way to the custody suite. Wilson had sat in Mark's office and allowed him to go and inform his Head of Department that he wouldn't be able to take his lectures and classes for a good while; in fact, he'd had to go to the common room to find Michael as it was the afternoon tea break. Usually he would have gone to sit with Sandra, Michael and whoever else from their department was around. The atmosphere had been different that day; it seemed news of his predicament and of his arrival with two police officers had already got around. Sandra pretended not to notice him and there was an embarrassed shuffling of papers and feet as he joined the group; even old Ernest wouldn't catch his eye. Michael had been away at a management meeting so Mark would have to call him later; sod the rest of them, he had thought, and wandered down to the postgrad room to see if Justine was there for him to try and explain again. She hadn't been and that had been it. He had never been back since being taken into custody later that afternoon; then the trial and getting on for six years of his life gone.

The day that he had cracked had been played back in his mind many times over the years of his imprisonment. He'd taken Justine out and told her he had something life-changing to tell her. For some reason he'd driven her to Stanmer Park and explained what he'd been doing and done and why and that it was all going to be sorted soon and they'd be together properly. Of course now, looking back, he realized he'd never expected her to react that way. She claimed their relationship, their passion, had never been about the money and because he obviously thought it was, she knew he didn't understand her and never would. It had floored him that she said she wanted to see other people anyway; but Justine wasn't a great liar and sure enough it emerged that she had already been seeing Tom and that she had become pretty fed up with Mark's developing obsession with his family, seemingly disregarding that the reason for it was now apparent and for her benefit as well. That had rather sealed it. He knew he'd acted out of character and in a sort of desperate panic to unburden himself, but Justine's reaction, showing her colours, must have been a kind of signal moment. He had had to accept that it had all been for nothing. He'd driven her back to the flat and once the shock of it had sunk in she had been decent enough to look pretty sad and to let him tell Fiona before going to the police. He'd got back home and after a pretty horrendous scene when he confessed to Fiona had called DI Wilson to say he had something sensational for him. Wilson had been busy and Mark didn't want to say too much to his assistant, so it hadn't been until the afternoon when he'd told the police and persuaded them to believe him.

No doubt the confession might be characterised as cathartic but he had felt he had no option and it was basically just making the most of it. He'd expected the publicity and scandal that accompanied the arrest and the trial four months later and had revelled in it at the time, but it had all fallen a little flat after the guilty plea and mandatory life sentence. Musing on it over the years, maybe he should have played it all out for the jury and press, however really he had little option to do that after confessing. Looking back on that last day with Justine he knew he should have realized that even before his arrest she had started to extricate herself from their situation. While it was fair enough of her to say she knew nothing about any of it all, he'd thought it rather disingenuous when she had made it clear the life of a well catered for mistress would never have been enough and anyway, as she'd told him, she didn't need the hassle that had surrounded their relationship from the start. In fact she'd been angry that he seemed to assume she was little more than a money-grasping whore. But it was also and mainly the moralistic posturing that had thrown him – sure enough, he hadn't included her in the planning but she'd pressed him to do something and to sort their lives out; and what the hell had she expected? She'd never turned down any of the trips away or the dresses or the free and easy lifestyle he'd provided.

He realized he should have known not to trust his old university friend Tom. They'd shared a lot together including the same interests in women and drugs. The first time they'd gone over to his inherited country house, he'd been flattered by the effect Justine had on his old mates: it was obvious Tom was interested but Mark had been too full of himself to think she'd prefer anyone else. Since then Tom had had his eye on her and he shouldn't have let his arrogance obscure the obvious. In fact he'd almost encouraged it, without having the sense to realize that Tom could afford it all and more without multiple murders.

Nonetheless, Justine and Tom had been something of a kick in the teeth – particularly as she had swanned off with Tom for a few weeks in the States without even waiting for the trial to commence. On reflection maybe the bigger shock was that he never saw it coming. The thing was that even with Justine out of the picture, Mark knew he couldn't face life with Fiona either, even if that had been an option – after all, there'd have been no need to murder her parents if that was to be the end result.

***

After being allocated to an open prison and in the months leading up to his possible parole, he had come to the decision to write about it – surely it deserved some recognition in any history of crime anthologies as a perfectly planned and carried out crime. More to the point, Gemma, the young probation officer who was writing her report on the viability of him being paroled, was obviously impressed with his story, and that was an avenue certainly worth exploring. From what he'd found out about her background, for Gemma the job was effectively just a little extra and to salve some sort of social conscience which by all accounts had been awoken through studying Sociology at Reading University for three years. (My God, he thought, his subject certainly had something to answer for.) There was certainly plenty of money in her family. Mark was used to managing classes and seminars and he'd engineered their meetings at Ford to focus more on her situation than his. He had found out the family had a big house in Farnham and had bought her a flat in Littlehampton, not that far from the prison. It had seemed to him that it was just time to tell all, and why not start with his probation officer? After all, it might help with the parole report – a few well-placed quotes demonstrating how he was facing up to it, coming clean, a fresh start and so on could do little harm. Then he could really go for it once he was out.

In fact, Mark had quite enjoyed the probation visits. Initially he had thought of the probation officer he was initially allocated as being an illustration of the perfect stereotype. David was an earnest, 'old school' style probation officer who was approaching retirement and clearly felt disillusioned by changes to the probation system, which, to him, seemed to be moving away from rehabilitation and re-integration towards an obsession with risk management. He had been convinced Mark was sorry to have thrown away his career as a bright young academic in the brave new world of the social sciences. Then somewhat out of the blue, and shortly after their first two sessions, David had decided to go part-time. While Mark certainly didn't feel he could take any credit for that, their second meeting had turned into a slightly incongruous role reversal with David talking about his training to be a lay preacher and needing two days a week with his family and the fact the job had turned out not to be what he thought he'd signed up for. Then in July on his goodbye visit, he'd brought his replacement along, the equally earnest but somewhat better looking do-gooder, Gemma. Mark had appreciated David's visits, he liked the fact that however misguided he might or might not be – and who was Mark to judge? – he did exude a genuineness and concern that was hard to see in so many of the officials Mark had dealt with since his arrest, starting with his legal team come to think of it. That last visit had been interesting: in spite of his calling to a more spiritual existence, David had clearly had difficulty in focusing on anything else apart from Gemma's legs, with a sort of doleful expression of what might have been. Mark had refrained from suggesting he would be happy to leave the room, get on with his hut cleaning job and leave them to it. He had sensed that Gemma was not completely unaware of her provocativeness, and quite enjoyed being in the meeting with two older – OK, he had to face that – and presumably slightly frustrated men. He recalled leaving that meeting quite looking forward to working on his parole application with her.

Since then, she'd visited just about every fortnight. He'd always thought it rather bizarre when he had heard of prisoners forming 'relationships' with different categories of prison visitors – he'd assumed it was those visitors, with nothing better to do than fill their presumably empty existences with some kind of vicarious excitement, who had initiated such liaisons. Maybe this was different or maybe he didn't want to feel that was happening here; the thing was, he'd got to quite look forward to their meetings – and at Ford it was all very civilized, un-supervised, tea and coffee and as long as they wanted. In the main, though, it had been because Gemma had apparently been somewhat star-struck – even after all those years he reckoned that the whole plan and its execution sounded a little classy.

Gemma had the look he hadn't seen for the last few years, one which had typified the faces of so many of his students a few years ago – a mix of naivety and freshness with a dash of wanting to change the world, all the while ignoring the reality that what they actually wanted was to get paired off and look a little glamorous. Perhaps that was a little unkind. Gemma had studied a Sociology degree, typically, and had a bit more about her than the few soft-arsed, hip types she'd no doubt had flings with while at university. Also, and particularly crucially, she was pretty stunning looking; and he was confident he was adept enough to play the experienced, older man. All in all it was ready-made for him; and beyond that glib appraisal of it all, which Mark knew was far too stereotypical, he liked Gemma, he liked good-looking, bright women. He didn't know what to expect and what issues he'd face when he eventually got out, and maybe it was just that he'd made the wrong decisions with rich in-laws and provocative students in the past; and that perhaps this could be a second chance to make the most of the class system. Anyway she wasn't a prison visitor only doing it to feel she was good; sure, she might be a do-gooder probation officer-cum-social worker, but at least it was part of her job and not just charity.

Gemma had started on her official role with Mark by trying to act and sound as professional as she could and as she'd been trained to.

'Let's start with your pre-prison life and how that might help explain why you're here.'

Well, there was nothing wrong with her following her mentor's notes and presumably some probation officer guidelines on how to get the right relationship with your clients. Here we go, he thought, let's start with my family and explain that I was not abused or treated in any other way than wonderfully, then keep Gemma happy by blaming drugs and the people I got in with. That would be good for her report, it would fit the theory she had no doubt picked up in her training.

'Well you know, I had a normal childhood, really quite idyllic, very loving, it was when I went to college the year before I got to university, everyone was trying out cannabis and LSD and I got involved with the wrong people. I was easily impressed back then. We thought drugs and love and peace could change the world.'

Gemma busily recorded it in her neat, pre-D'Nealian-style handwriting, Zaner-Boser style he thought it was called, that reflected both her age and schooling.

'Thing is, I don't think that explained my crimes. I got over that soon after I got to university, after my first year at Kent when I really got into Sociology. You know, I think I got disillusioned with the hippy thing and gradually became just greedy and materialistic.'

He thought he should try to appeal to their common interest in Sociology.

'Like I said, when I was at Kent, I was really inspired by studying a subject which was alive and spoke to the real world, it was like a veil was lifting from my very being; some of the insights from some of the theorists and the research from ethnographers, how they linked the micro with the macro.'

Well so what if it was sounding like another lecture, and if he was laying it on with a massive helping of flannel? Thinking back to when he'd taken his first degree, he'd only ever attended enough lectures and classes to keep the department tutors off his back. In reality, he'd been somewhat amazed at the enthusiasm shown for some of the most obvious ideas and had enough confidence that he could write with the necessary coherence to get to dash off the required essays as and when they arrived due. In fact, a couple of books from the library and a handful of blues or dexxies had been enough for him to get a reasonable 2:1 degree; and come to think of it, not that many books had been needed for the string of consciousness programme that was classed as the sociology of culture course – drugs and a bit of imagination seemed to do the trick. The thing was, he had actually liked a lot of his time as a student, and while the content and ideas and so on meant little he loved the attendant lifestyle around academia, the way students and tutors got on with each other as equals, or so he'd thought at the time. The late-night films in the lecture theatre, the drugs and bands in the union bar and the girls; the whole thing was all so cool. In fact, thinking back he had actually believed that lecturing and all the resultant perks would make a pretty decent sort of future for him; and that had been the case of course, it hadn't been a bad way of earning status and a living. It just hadn't matched his requirements at the time; and to some extent it was Justine and maybe his better-off friends too who had ensured that was the case.

He continued on with his impression management cloaked as unburdening, continuing with the theme of the importance of a sociological understanding and imagination.

'In particular, it was sociologists like Steven Box, Stan Cohen and Laurie Taylor who really showed me how exciting research and writing can be; and as I got to know them and the others we swapped ideas and they didn't treat you as inferior. It was quite a time to be student, we even met up with them and other tutors in the union bar after departmental seminars, it was pretty cool.'

It seemed to Mark that Gemma was obviously and easily impressed.

'Oh, I read their book *Psychological Survival* on my degree course, it was amazing, and you knew them, that's amazing.'

Mark applied some selective memory.

'After my undergraduate course they took me on as a research student and it was then that I realized my dream and after some part-time tutoring at Kent, the job at Sussex came along; you know, Stan Cohen even wrote my reference for it.'

It might not have been quite like that but the basics were there and why not embellish them? He had had enough of this part of his life and as far as he was concerned more than paid his dues. He knew he could get Gemma to help him and he could see it might not be difficult to persuade her that he could help her too.

'The thing was, Gemma – may I call you that?'

She had blushed, crossed her legs (always a good sign) and said she could see he was different from most of the hapless and hopeless cases, even if she didn't label them as such, that she had been introduced to in her training and probationary year, so why not? Mark had ploughed on, he knew he mustn't get carried away and make it too obvious or too soon. If there was one thing the last few years had impressed on him, it was patience and the need to adopt a different approach to time.

'I became greedy and I started to forget why I had been so enthused by the academic life and to act like I was pretty important and also, you know, that I realized how easy it was to use my status to indulge myself. I could see that quite a few of the young female students were enthralled a little and I took to seducing those I could tell would be grown up enough about it. Actually it got to the stage where, with increasing regularity, my office door was locked and one or other of my students would be on my knee or over the desk or, most usually and I found quite surprising, just opening my jeans and taking things from there. It was tempting and I let myself be tempted: no excuses, I'm afraid.'

That was far enough for the time being. He didn't want to get Gemma worried about inappropriate relationships with her clients– she was new to the job and would have had the rules and regs foisted on her through her training courses. Keep it to a nice balance of contriteness and awareness of where 'I went wrong', along with some obvious titillation. Mark sensed she was the sort who'd get quite horny thinking about her days as a student and the lecturers she'd probably fancied. He would have to judge when to pull the stops out. She looked nice and fresh but it was more than that, there was something else about her that had got to him. She looked like she would be fun to be with, even if that after more than five years without sex with anyone apart from himself his judgement might be a little clouded. Time for a little flattery.

'I'm actually a little sad to say all of this, and you know you're the first person I feel I can talk like this to. Of course I have realized that what I did was absolutely appalling and I am more ashamed than you could imagine, but having you to open up to about the reasons for it is something I've missed and something I need now.'

Even if it was pretty blatant, Mark was surprised at how easy it was to turn oneself into a project; but there was also an element of truth in it all which added to the plausibility. Although some of his companions over the last few years might have been intelligent, they were all, and to a man too of course, absolutely self-centred. The one trait common to all the prisoners he'd mixed with. Mark pushed on with the confessional.

'I lost sight of the importance and privilege of my position – and you know, Gemma, it's so refreshing to be able to talk to someone without trying to impress them or grovel to their petty shows of authority. I'm not saying that all the prison officers have been like that, some have been fine, but a lot of them are resentful of people like me you know, and a lot of them are pretty thick too.'

He thought he'd best avoid being too critical.

'But it's so nice just to be able to use your name; and I feel you're going to be really good at your job and as well as that be really good for me too'

He'd noticed her smile, redden and look down; he knew he was getting the balance right, and that he hadn't lost it either. This was the first time he'd tried his seduction techniques in a long while.

'Anyway, I lost the plot as they say and ended up getting involved with a particular student – so much so that we became regular lovers – her freedom and openness showed me what I'd been missing in my own home life.'

No harm in setting the bar reasonably high he thought.

'She gave me everything for a time, I'd never had sex like it. She was compliant but somehow assertive at the same time; she made me feel like I was a great lover, the best. Is it alright for me to talk like this?'

He didn't wait for an answer, he had clued up enough on probation and social work training to know that encouraging absolute openness from the client was deemed a good thing, how the 'truth' had to be brought out, however bizarre or horrific it might prove to be.

'The thing was, she wanted more than being a dark secret – and to be fair she deserved so much more.'

He noticed that Gemma had just about given up taking notes.

'I guess I felt trapped; she, Justine to give her her name, was too good to lose, I felt, and I knew I had to do something to keep her. As you may have read my ex-wife's family were very rich and the rest is history as they say. It sounds like an excuse and I'm not claiming that, but I got caught up in a situation that got out of hand. I let my passion run away. In fact I became a different person, I became obsessed and obsessive.'

He had to convince Gemma from the start that he was not the sort of criminal likely to re-offend or be a danger to the public. Once that was established he was pretty sure that he could help her make his case for release on parole. He'd read up on it all, and had even managed to persuade David to give him a copy of the probation training course programme before he'd left the job. In a nutshell, show a decent amount of remorse, accept you deserved the punishment, were ashamed and wanted now to show you had learnt and were willing to contribute to society. Always a matter of balance.

Of course one issue would be what he'd do in future; and Gemma didn't yet realize he intended her to have a big role in that too.

'This has been so helpful Gemma, I hope you can stay on my case 'cos I'm sure you'll be able to help me and help me regain myself and pride again, and, let's be honest, my desires too, after all I'm still young enough.' He couldn't resist it.

He could see Gemma was intrigued and realized it had to be set up as a sort of challenge for her too. She took the invite as a compliment and said she'd look forward to helping him through everything.

'Maybe next time we can go into the crime and your confession – which will be a very positive aspect of the case and my report too.'

He walked to the gatepost with her – so much more civilized in the prison camp atmosphere down here at Ford. It wasn't yet quite appropriate to part with a hug but he remembered thinking that might not be too far away.

***

After his probation visit from Gemma, Mark had wandered across the site and back to his afternoon job in the gardens. He'd wanted to keep reasonably fit and it had been surprisingly easy down here. Apart from the gym in the evening, free-time association period, working with the gardening teams had helped him keep in shape. The work itself had involved digging trenches to secure the metal frames for the poly tunnels, constructing them and then general weeding and tending of the vegetables, mainly cucumber and tomatoes, that they grew for the prison kitchen and beyond. Over the years he'd had a few prison jobs, there had been hut cleaning in the afternoons when he'd finished in the prison library or the education block, which he'd managed to swap for working with one of the gardening teams at the start of the summer. The gardening and growing were supervised by civilian staff, 'civvies', who each had a team of four to six inmates. His team had included a couple of older prisoners, one a self-employed jeweller who'd run a small shop in Hatton Gardens and made a fortune, or so he claimed, from selling fake stuff and fiddling his taxes, and old Jim who'd been involved in 'long firm' frauds for years and had finally come unstuck. Those two did little of the actual gardening and their main task focused on sorting the tea breaks in the little hut they kept their tools in and then regaling him, Jeff their 'civvy' and the two East London lads who'd not got very far as apprentices to a car 'ringing' syndicate, with tales of the high life they'd led in West London in the early and mid-60s. Jeff, the supposed supervisor of the 'team' had been easily impressed and had seemed keener on the tea breaks than on keeping his gang to the task. Mark had always found it mildly amusing how so many prisoners, and particularly the white-collar ones, were forever showing off about how well they'd done and how much money they'd made before their time inside. There was no apparent sense of irony with telling tales of living the high life and travelling the world, while waiting for their prison meals of bread and somewhat tasteless corn beef and potato mash, or of drinking their tea from large urns and in enamel mugs. It seemed it was a matter of pride to make sure it was known that it had all been worthwhile.

Anyway the work had helped keep Mark fit and he'd enjoyed helping construct the poly huts and then seeing the cucumbers growing and then being harvested, if that was the word, and made ready for selling to local suppliers. In fact he had become quite an expert in the cultivation of cucumbers and tomatoes too.

So he felt in pretty good shape, in fact a good deal more so than before his sentence. It wasn't that he wanted the ridiculously inverted shape of some of the body builder types, just to be lean and fit-looking. My goodness, he thought, there were likely to be some super-fit ex-cons around for the next few years after the work they'd put in in the weight room. And apparently the police training had got easier, so maybe the balance in relation to physical fitness was moving toward favouring the criminal, he mused.

***

The thing with prison life was to keep your counsel – he was due to play backgammon with Graham and John later and, as throughout their time and (in some ways) friendship at Ford, they never talked about their plans for the outside. The Londoners who knew one another, the Jack-the-lads, the car ringers and so on enjoyed showing off, they did their time while plotting strategies and picking up hints and contacts. They maintained their front at all costs. Although they worked with the petty criminals and regulars in the working units and teams and listened unavoidably to the constant bragging of what and who they'd done, Mark and the other white-collar offenders, fraudsters and long termers were of a different mind. They didn't see their crimes in career terms – maybe life-changing but certainly not part of a lifestyle. Their criminal activities were to afford a certain lifestyle, not to *be* a lifestyle, there was no social element with them: there was not a real, subcultural, gang style of life with corporate crime, fraud, or with one-off murdering for that matter. They really didn't fit the criminological theorising of his previous existence.

Apart from his parents and brother and a couple of colleagues from Sussex, Mark had decided at the start of his sentence to cut himself off from the majority of his previous friends and contacts. It had been easier because of Justine's obvious intent from the day he confessed to have nothing to do with him, and then Tom's decision to take her on himself. He hadn't wanted his parents or brother to visit but had kept in touch with the odd letter, and, maybe a little unkindly, he felt that the few visitors from university he'd had seemed to be more interested in being able to bask in a sort of reflected glory that came from knowing a serial killer, rather than offering any particular support to him.

Now it was time to start again, and as he kept reminding himself he was only 32. For the first time in years he could see there would be an end to this. Over the last few years, all Mark had read and thought about had made it clear that if he was going to make up for the dead time it would have to be through gaining access to the world of privilege – and this time not necessarily by way of chemistry and murder. Rather through acting, charm and a dash of hedonism perhaps, along with the lure of an intriguing and dangerous past. That wasn't to say that poison and murder might not still have their uses and place; it would be a last resort this time around, though.

Mark felt better in himself that at last he had a project to work on. He had not thought in any great detail about post-prison life, aside from writing some kind of memoir, and maybe becoming a kind of criminal celebrity in the manner of the Krays or the Great Train Robbers. However, that course of action offered no guarantees: the Krays were in prison for the foreseeable anyway, and the train robbers either in exile or penury. He knew of a few ex-cons who had moved into quasi-social work or self-help-type roles but that wasn't for him. Most notable perhaps was John McVicar, a former armed robber who'd been paroled a couple of years back, somewhat ironically after completing a Sociology degree during his time inside, and who had since written his autobiography which had already led to a recently released film based on his life. That probably wasn't for him though, and Gemma offered a real and pretty pleasant alternative possibility.

Also it wouldn't necessarily have to be completely calculating – Gemma genuinely appeared a good bet, both looks wise (the *sine qua non*), but also as a person to spend time with. Almost unwittingly he'd started the process and plan at their first official meeting by themselves. It had become absolutely clear from a couple of questions he'd asked about her school days and holidays that Gemma had a fairly privileged background and upbringing, and that the lifestyle she had was certainly not down to her salary as a junior probation officer. He had found out she was an only child and that her dad had been in the diplomatic service but had died from cancer, quite suddenly and in his early fifties. So that offered the opportunity for a new strategy for him, and Mark knew his next step would be to get to know a little more detail about her current family situation. It was always easy enough to steer their discussion about his future and rehabilitation into some concerned discussion of her family and future career prospects, and perhaps of the difficulties and pressures of being a rich kid.

Running it through his mind in the hours and hours spent with little better to do, it did, unarguably, sound calculating and dispassionate but that wasn't really a fair reflection of how he felt. He certainly wanted to make up for lost time and to have access to the lifestyle he'd touched on and almost achieved, but he wanted to do it with someone he cared for and someone who cared for him. Like most of his peers at Ford, he felt he deserved and had earned some time with the finer things and Gemma had got to him, albeit in a different way than Justine. There was no way she would be another Fiona either, but maybe she would provide access to what he still felt he deserved from life and this time he would be doing it with her and for them both. He'd make sure he didn't get things so spectacularly wrong again.

Even after Gemma's second visit Mark had found himself almost counting the days till the next one; and while that was partly because he had a plan of action to develop it was also that he was starting to feel Gemma was someone he could have a good time with. Without making it too obvious he had confirmed that, as expected, she had a pretty well-off family, and that, really quite conveniently, it had been as a result of her father dying and leaving a considerable insurance pay-out plus the large family house in Surrey to his widow, Gemma's mother. Indeed, that was close to a perfect scenario – even more so when Gemma told him she had come along late in her parents' marriage, when they'd all but given up hope of any offspring. So, an ageing mother, pottering around in a large mock farmhouse in Farnham...

What's happening to me? Mark pondered, as he checked the value of house prices in the Sussex and South London areas in the different local papers he'd asked old Neville, the red band, so supposedly trusted prisoner, in the library, to get for him. If they were going to be together they (this time he and Gemma) would need to sell her family house. There were still the odd moments of doubt – he'd woken up early that morning wondering if he really was some kind of compulsive killer – but they could always be rationalised. After all, he got so close last time; and to do it again, and with a known and well publicised history, that would have to go down as pretty impressive.

Yes, it was a plan, a direction again and a project, and something to keep him focused in the next few weeks while waiting on the parole board's decision. Mark knew it would not be an immediate release even though it was the second time around. If he could get a date, maybe a month or so after the probable knock-back, that would definitely be acceptable. A date between the second and third parole opportunities was common practice and, from what he'd been able to find out, it was usually quite often soon after the second one. Meanwhile he had to convince Gemma that any social conscience and desire to do good things by way of working for the probation service might be okay for a short time but was not the calling she seemed to believe it was. And neither was it the life he intended them to have together.

Although he'd enjoyed the work with the gardening team that summer and into early autumn, he felt it was time for a change before his hoped for parole – he'd put in a request to the SO that had been approved pretty much straightaway. Mark had never fancied or applied for a kitchen job but it appeared it was different in an open prison, with much more freedom to experiment and bring in different produce. He'd never applied because it was clearly not the ideal job for a convicted poisoner, but he'd been there a good time now and was generally viewed as pretty much rehabilitated. On the whole, the officers liked him: he was no trouble and never treated them as lesser beings in the way some of the long firm fraudsters and other corporate criminals did. He'd made a point of trying to keep as many of the officers and inmates as possible on-side. Anyway, he wasn't planning to poison the prison population at Ford, but he wanted to check out the properties of peach stones and the best ways of disguising the bitter tastes that characterised most natural poisons. It might even be therapeutic to keep his hand in and, while one never knew, he might need to come up with a slightly different way of freeing Gemma and him from his potential future mother-in-law.

As it was, his life moved on in its usual disconnected manner as the days shortened and cold evenings crept in towards the seond half of October. With release on the horizon he just had to stay patient and keep on with the natural pace of institutional living. He had helped Gemma produce his probation report and the results of the parole board were due imminently, and certainly by the middle of November, and he still felt pretty confident. Last time, six months ago in May, the PO had called him in and said it was a close call but they felt he needed to work with the probation team to ensure he had a strategy for when he was released on licence. Furthermore, Mark was well aware that maybe another few months would in any case satisfy natural justice and proportionality and any potential media-orchestrated 'holier than thou' comments. Mark had wondered if he had interpreted the signs correctly, but there'd been a strong hint that even if he wasn't given immediate release it would be within a month or two at the most. He'd been to the various interviews and had been working with, not to mention on, the probation team, which was now just Gemma plus the occasional supervisory visit from her new boss, another David, basically to check how she was doing. After all, he didn't feel anyone could realistically call him a danger to society.

It was strange how his parole officer was becoming his future, even if she didn't realize it. Anyway, it was well into October and it was time for him to get back into 'doing' mode. Gemma was due to visit on either Monday the 20th or the next day – an odd visit, as the report was done, but she seemed keen to see him which was presumably a good thing. He knew he needed to start things moving.

Sure enough, he got a call from the Gate Officer at 11.00 on the Monday letting him know he had a probation visit. Graham and John had a fair idea what he was up to, they all knew they had a good chance of parole before the end of the year or at least early in the next one and had spent the last couple of evenings discussing ways of keeping their probation officers happy when on licence, which was a licence for life for him as a lifer, but in the case of the others only till the end of their sentences. He'd hinted to Graham he intended to keep Gemma on his case – and to do it both officially and not. Graham had seen Gemma leaving the other day and agreed she looked pretty good and had joked that she might be worth him considering 'reverting to type' as he rather crudely put it. Graham was nothing if not thoughtful.

Mark strolled across to the special interview room. Gemma wasn't in her usual slacks and sweater, he'd never seen her in a suit and could see the buttons of her white blouse just about managing to pull together. She smiled, 'They're letting me take the lead in court this afternoon …'

'Well it suits you, you look great, and thanks for coming and with all your help I really think I'm going to be out before Christmas and I wanted to ask you something so I'm really glad you came.'

He needed to be more daring, and my God she did look good, the top buttons of her blouse were open enough to reveal a hint of cleavage, and he could see the shape of her breasts through the light cotton. It was difficult to keep his eyes away. Gemma sat back and got her notebook ready. He decided to take the lead.

'Thing is and I know I've mentioned this but I was wondering if you have managed to do anything about being my probation contact and support when I do eventually get parole. I've felt good with you since I've been down here and to be honest I'd like to see more of you anyway, even without the professional contact if you know what I mean.'

Ok it was a bit of a leap but unless he'd lost his hold on reality altogether, he was pretty confident. He ploughed on.

'Look, I know it may not be easy to arrange but surely there's some value in continuity and building a relationship.'

He could see she was flattered.

'Yes I'd like that and I'll put it to David when I get back in the office, but I do know other officers who have continued to work with licensed parolees. And I think it's seen as good policy at the moment.'

That was enough for now, he'd leave suggesting she take a few years off and go and live a bit until they'd actually got the formalities sorted out and a date for his release set. He turned to what he'd do once on parole.

'You know I have got some money behind me, I won't be starting out again with nothing. I'd like to rent a place down here around Arundel somewhere. When Fiona sold our house in 1978 and moved back to her family's home I got my legitimate share of that and of course have had it saved since then, not much choice there really.'

There was no harm in reminding Gemma that he wasn't a dead loss. Perhaps in retrospect it hadn't been the best time to sell, as the £14,000 or so they'd got in late 1975 would have been nearer £25,000 now, but on the other hand Gordon had brought it for them so there was no mortgage to pay off – and they'd have got a few thousand less if she hadn't waited for six months after the trial before selling it. He had been a little surprised Fiona hadn't tried to keep it all but his solicitor had assured him that as they were married and joint owners he would get half. Anyway, Fiona had sole ownership of her family's pile overlooking the Channel and that put the £7,000 he got into perspective; and also she'd been quite open to agreeing that he got a small percentage of Gordon's savings as well. His solicitor had done well on that side of things, managing to get him around eight per cent of his in-laws' estate minus the value of the house itself of course; but then they were married and feminism hadn't come on that far. So overall and given the interest rates, there was a decent amount in the bank, must be close on or just over fifty thousand, he reckoned.

'I know that, Mark, and I know you've got the skills and intelligence to start again.'

There was no harm in coming over as a little vulnerable and in need of bit of looking after.

'With your help, Gemma.'

It was the second time he'd used her name and she didn't flinch. He knew it was best to leave things while she thought about it, but he did ask her if she'd come down to see him when he got the parole result. He appealed to her sense of duty too.

'It isn't going to be so straightforward after so many years away but, you know, I think we'll do well together.'

Maybe it wasn't quite time to put his arm round her but he sensed a tension and excitement as he got up and wished her well for the court appearance. He told her again she looked a million dollars, and in a way and with a look that surely she could hardly mistake.

'I think I'm ready to go and I think she's ready for it too,' he confided to Graham and John as he got back to the education block and the end of their morning's studying. As usual Graham was supportive as well as slightly amused.

'Well you deserve a bit of luck.'

John just smiled: 'One thing I've learned is that people don't change that much.'

Mark spent the rest of the afternoon thinking about his strategy for life after all of this, and for Gemma. Once he'd got a date and time frame, he'd get her to talk about her own life and plans and then point out to her how and why she could do so much if she wanted to; and how it would be good to do it with him of course. He knew she was single so a good angle would be to pretend to encourage her to find a suitable man. He could take on the role of a sort of supportive pimp, suggest she go on a few dates, then he'd gently put down whoever had rolled into her life and convince Gemma she was too good for them, they weren't right for her and so on. So he'd help sort her life and future out even though he'd make sure she believed it was the other way around and she was the social worker. A simple and familiar tale would unfold and surely those were the most reliable. She'd be absolutely ready for him to save her from a series of unsuitable and unsatisfactory flings. Meanwhile he'd have spent time with her and engineered meeting and winning over her mother and any other family and friends; and perhaps a good plan might even be to let her show him off as her project.

During the latter part of the afternoon he had returned to cleaning the older huts he was still assigned to in addition to his recent move to the kitchens. After a little desultory dusting he wandered back to his own room in the newer block. He had a little time before the working groups came back from the other side of the prison site to change from their work overalls before tea. He sat back on his bed and let his mind wander back to Jean – maybe Gemma's mother would take to him too. He thought back to the pre-Justine days. It was amazing how the details still played so clearly in his mind. It had all looked very clear-cut then: he was a young university lecturer with a rich family – of in-laws, admittedly. He'd had plenty of opportunities to indulge himself. If he'd played it all a little differently, how might it have been? Mark knew that this time it had to be gone through with the utmost care and attention, this time it would have to work out for good. This time he wouldn't misjudge things and people quite so spectacularly and wouldn't hanker after any theatrical moments and self-publicity. This time he'd be with the rich girl herself, rather than using her as the go-between for another Justine. He'd rent a place near Gemma's flat for a while anyway, but not too close; maybe he could persuade Gemma to do some looking around on his behalf. He wandered across to the library; he needed to get a map of Sussex and then check Gemma's address next time she came.

PART FIVE – EPILOGUE

November 28 1980

'I can't believe you came to meet me, you've already done so much to help me get sorted.'

It was the day of his release, albeit on licence. He sat back in Gemma's little MG Midget looking back as they drove past the fencing and gardens surrounding Ford Open Prison and then the row of prison officers' houses. The white sports car absolutely suited her: not too flash, but adding enough glamour to suggest she had more about her, and more money around her, than might fit the stereotypical junior probation officer.

Mark had served over five and half years since confessing to poisoning both of his in-laws. He was lucky to be getting out so soon and before Christmas too, but then he'd played the system, he'd been a model inmate and he'd secured unswerving support from the probation service – in his case and conveniently in the form of Gemma, now allocated as his particular contact and case worker.

'Well, I wanted to show you the flat I've sorted for you; and it's not far from my place in Littlehampton so it's no trouble.'

Mark had persuaded Gemma to take him on after his release as his probation support and, probably not following procedures, he'd given her access to his money to sort a flat for him on his release. Money he'd accrued from the divorce settlement from his very wealthy ex-wife, somewhat ironically as a result of the death (or more correctly murder by him) of her parents. It was all falling into place, but there was something else too. Mark was really quite excited about getting to know Gemma, and not just because of her clearly privileged background: he genuinely thought he could have a good time with her if he managed it right this time. After all, he was only 32, just seven years older than her, and he'd looked after himself, especially once he'd been allocated to the open prison, played a little football and cricket and done some running. And she was bloody attractive; she looked great today in a cropped pullover and tight jeans that hugged her firm figure.

'Look, let me take you for a meal later, I want to say thanks and more than anything I want you to see me away from prison visiting rooms. You know I'm going to find it odd living here, not knowing people, trying to get my career started again. I don't want to presume on you too much but I think you must know that I do really like you.'

He sensed her tighten her grip on the steering wheel and imagined her blushing. That was enough for now: he knew that she was interested. He'd have to convince her it was fine to separate their professional ties from the rest. He sensed it would be easy enough too. And he had time at last.

'Yes that'd be nice. I'll show you some of the few sights of the town.'

'OK, let's go and look at where you've got me to stay; and we can catch up on everything later. Mind you, I have been following the news though; it's amazing really, a former film star of sorts becoming the new American President by all accounts. That's quite a contrast with the new Labour leader Michael Foot; imagine Reagan and Foot as leaders of the free world, if we ever get rid of Thatcher of course.'

Although he had a decent amount of money from his divorce settlement with Fiona, Mark was aware it wouldn't last forever. It wasn't that he was desperate to continue with his second career but Gemma's situation meant that it was a definite option; and he had, after all, learnt a good deal from his ultimately unsuccessful pursuit of Justine.